MOUNTAIN JACK PIKE

ST. LOUIS FIRE

#6

Also by Robert J. Randisi

Angel Eyes
#2: Death's Angel
#3: Wolf Pass
#4: Chinatown Justice
#5: Logan's Army
#6: Bullets and Bad Times
#7: Six-Gun Angel
#8: Avenging Angel
#9: Angel for Hire

Tracker
#1: The Winning Hand
#2: Lincoln County
#3: The Blue Cut Job
#4: Chinatown Chance
#5: The Oklahoma Score

Mountain Jack Pike
#1: Mountain Jack Pike
#2: Rocky Mountain Kill
#3: Comanche Come-On
#4: Crow Bait
#5: Green River Hunt
#6: St. Louis Fire
#7: The Russian Bear
#8: Hard for Justice
#9: Henry Lee Lucas
#10: Bull's Eye Blood
#11: Deep Canyon Kill
#12: Fire in the Hole

MOUNTAIN JACK PIKE

ST. LOUIS FIRE

#6

Robert J. Randisi

SPEAKING VOLUMES, LLC
NAPLES, FLORIDA
2012

St. Louis Fire #6

ISBN 978-1-61232-597-2

PROLOGUE

It wasn't Pike's first train ride.

The first one, however, was years before when, as a young man, he first came west.

Next to him, Skins McConnell was nervous.

It was his first train ride.

"Tain't natural," McConnell muttered.

"Relax."

"Thing could blow up at any minute."

"The engine is all the way in front, Skins," Pike said. "Even if it did explode, it's unlikely we'd be hurt."

"A horse is the only natural way to travel."

"Relax, Skins," Pike said, again. "Going to St. Louis by horseback would have taken forever."

Pike had been chosen by the other mountain men and trappers at the most recent rendezvous to go to St. Louis to try to talk some sense into the heads of the various fur companies. Of late, the prices they were willing to pay for skins and pelts had come down drastically, and the mountain men were in danger of having to find another way to make a living.

Pike was supposed to persuade them to pay more . . .

*   *   *

"I can't go," Pike had complained.

"Why not?" Jim Bridger had asked.

"I'd feel like a fish out of water, Jim," Pike said. "I ain't been to the city in years."

"But you *come* from the city," Bridger argued. "You'd feel less out of place than any of us."

"Still—"

"Also, you can talk."

"You can talk," Pike pointed out.

"I can't go."

"That's what I said."

"No," Bridger said, "I really can't go. I have a meeting with the army. They need me to do some negotiations with the Blackfeet."

"I'll take the Blackfeet," Pike said, "you take the city."

"Pike—"

"All right, all right," Pike said. "I'll go, but I won't enjoy it."

"We've taken up a collection," Bridger said. "We have enough for you and one other person to go."

"One other?"

"We thought it would keep you from getting lonely if you brought someone with you."

"A woman?"

"That's up to you," Bridger said, smiling.

"No, I guess not," Pike said. "I guess I'll give Skins a chance to see the big city."

"No," McConnell said, when Pike extended his invitation.

"Why not?"

"I ain't no city slicker."

"Well, neither am I."

"I won't go."

6

"Come on, Skins," Pike said. "It'll be a new adventure."

"I get enough adventure up here."

And so Skins McConnell had been adamant about not going—at first—but Pike would not give up that easily. He was not going to suffer the city alone when he could bring a good friend along.

"Skins," he said, making it up as he went along, "just think of the food, the liquor . . . and the women."

The last one was the one that got him.

"Women?"

"All pale skinned and golden haired," Pike said, laying it on thick.

"Red hair, too?"

"Of course," Pike said. "Blond, brown, red . . ."

"And pale skin?"

"White," Pike said, "absolutely white, and soft and scented—"

"And you'll know your way around?"

"We won't get lost," Pike said, which had been an evasive answer. Even though Pike had come from the east originally, he had never been to St. Louis.

"Well," McConnell said, "maybe it *would* be an adventure. Besides, somebody's got to keep you out of trouble."

"Sure," Pike said. "Coming?"

McConnell nodded.

"I'm coming."

"If I had known that we were going to travel this way—" McConnell complained.

"Look at that woman," Pike said, interrupting his friend.

"Where?" McConnell asked, still scowling.

"Across the aisle, about three rows up," Pike said, "walking toward us."

The woman was walking toward them, a tall, pale,

blond woman. She stopped two rows ahead of them and sat down. Her blond hair was plentiful, cascading down her back in shimmering waves.

"Good God," McConnell said. "Do you see that golden hair?"

"I see it."

"Think she'd appreciate some company?"

"I don't see why not?"

"You want to try?"

Pike shook his head.

"After you," he said. "I have to figure out what I'm going to say to the company owners."

"Well, all right," McConnell said, rising and stepping into the aisle. "If I'm not back soon—"

"I won't come looking for you," Pike said.

McConnell grinned and said, "Thanks."

Pike laid his head against the back of his seat and thought about the mountains. He missed them already, and couldn't wait to return to them, but what would happen if he returned in defeat. If the fur companies refused to bring their prices back up—ah, but what if they did? Soon the beaver wouldn't just be scarce, they'd be gone and then it wouldn't matter what the companies were ready to pay for beaver pelt. Buffalo skins, on the other hand, would be around for quite a while. They were much too plentiful to be wiped out by a few buffalo hunters and mountain men.

Weren't they?

So that made the trip worth making, and the price of fur worth fighting for.

He opened his eyes and saw McConnell returning, looking crestfallen.

"Back so soon?"

McConnell sat down and assumed his previous scowl.

"What happened?"

"She said her husband preferred that she travel alone," he said, dejectedly.

"You can't be mad at me because she's married," Pike said.

McConnell gave him a baleful stare.

"When we get to St. Louis, there'll be plenty of unmarried women."

"Promises, promises . . ." McConnell said.

PART ONE

THE CITY

CHAPTER ONE

When the train pulled into the station McConnell happily leaped from the train, happy to be standing on firm ground again.

"Let's head for the nearest watering hole," McConnell said, shouldering his pack.

"A hotel, first," Pike said. "We'll need a room, and a bath."

"A bath?" McConnell said. "You didn't say anything about a bath."

"We're in the city now, Skins," Pike said. "We'll be coming into contact with a lot of people. It wouldn't do for us to smell like . . ."

"Like what?"

"Like a couple of mountain men," Pike said. "Come on, let's find a buggy."

"For what?"

"To take us to a hotel."

"Can't we walk?"

"If we knew where one was, we could walk," Pike said. "When we find a cab, we'll let the driver take us to a nice hotel."

"With a bathtub?"

"With lots of bathtubs, I'm sure."

McConnell was intimidated by the sheer size of St. Louis. There were more buildings in one place than he'd ever seen before, and a hell of a lot more people than he'd ever seen. He felt crowded in, just riding through the streets in the buggy.

The ride wasn't bad in the beginning. The buildings they passed were simple homes, one story, small, some with fences around them. Later, they passed a shanty town, all tents and open fires.

"Now that doesn't look too bad," McConnell said.

As they moved closer to the city the buildings suddenly became larger, more modern. First some one-story structures, clean new wood, then two-story buildings, some parts newer than others, as if the second story had been added later. When they were among the three- and four-story buildings, stone and brick, McConnell really began to get edgy.

Pike had told the buggy driver that they needed a moderately priced hotel, and the man said he knew just the place. McConnell wished they'd hurry up and get there. The buildings were getting higher, and the streets even more crowded.

"Stop fidgeting," Pike said.

"I don't think this was such a good idea after all," McConnell said.

"Why not?"

"There are too many damned people here, Pike," McConnell said. "And these buildings get any higher they're gonna fall over. It ain't natural."

"You gettin' spooked, Skins?"

"Yeah," McConnell said. "I guess I am . . . kind of."

"Then we'll just try and wrap this up as soon as possible," Pike said. "There are three major fur companies here in St. Louis."

"Which one we gonna try first?"

"Hudson Bay, I guess," Pike said. "They're the biggest. Then North American. After that we'll go over to the Rocky Mountain Company."

"Can we do it all in one day?" McConnell asked.

Pike laughed.

"I doubt it, but we can try," Pike said. "Don't forget, we don't have appointments or anything. People in business in the city, they don't like to see other people without an appointment."

The buggy finally pulled up in front of a hotel that had three floors on it.

"Jesus," McConnell said, "that's the biggest hotel I ever seen."

"When's the last time you even saw a real hotel that wasn't a tent?" Pike asked, slapping his friend on the back heartily.

"Never."

"Come on," Pike said, "it won't bite."

As they walked from the buggy to the hotel Pike knew what his friend was feeling. He was also feeling crowded in by the number of people who were simply walking the street. His stomach was jumpy and he longed for some elbow room. He looked up at the sky and felt a moment's respite. It looked much the same, but when you were in the mountains you felt like you could touch the sky. Here there was no such feeling.

"What's the matter?" McConnell asked.

"The same thing that's the matter with you, Skins," Pike said. "I miss the mountains."

"How come you don't look as nervous as I do?"

"I'm better at hiding it."

They entered the hotel and walked to the front desk. They both had their clothes in canvas sacks, and the clerk gave them a look that travelled right down

15

his nose.

"Can I help you?" he asked. His tone and the look on his face said that he doubted he could.

"We need a room."

"A room?"

"One room," Pike said, "two beds."

The clerk didn't move. Suddenly, he was intimidated by the sheer size of the two men—especially Pike.

"You have a room like that, don't you?" Pike asked. "With two beds?"

"Well . . . of course."

"And a bathtub?"

"We have tubs on each floor."

"Not in the rooms?"

"You did say you wanted a moderately priced hotel, remember?" McConnell said.

"Oh, that's right," Pike said. He looked at the clerk and said, "Can we have a key, please?"

"Sure," the clerk said. "Room twelve, on the second floor."

"Fine," Pike said. "Have a couple of those bathtubs filled with hot water, will you?"

"Yes . . . sir."

"We'll be ready in about fifteen minutes," Pike said, picking up his canvas bag. McConnell had never put his down, standing there with it slung over his shoulder. The two mountain men had drawn a lot of attention in the lobby. They were not the usual type who walked the streets of St. Louis, and stayed in the hotels.

"The baths will be ready, sir."

"Good."

They both turned and suddenly a dozen people found something else to look at.

"What are they lookin' at?" McConnell asked as they went up the stairs to the second floor.

"I guess they've never seen a couple of real mountain men before," Pike said.

"We gonna have to put up with that the whole time we're here?" McConnell said. "Bad enough we got to be here, I ain't gonna put up with bein' stared at."

"Well," Pike said, "the first step to keeping that from happening is taking a bath."

"Oh yeah," McConnell said, "a bath."

"After that," Pike said, "we'll work on the rest."

"The rest?"

"Maybe a shave, a haircut, some new clothes—"

"Wait a minute," McConnell said. "Where's all the money for this gonna come from?"

"This may be a big city," Pike said, "but they still must play poker."

The room was fairly large, compared to the tents they were used to sharing in the mountains—when they had tents. There were two beds and enough floor space for them to sleep if they found the mattresses too soft. McConnell dropped his sack on one of the beds and sat next to it.

Pike went to the window and found that it overlooked the street in front of the hotel.

"I need a drink and something to eat," McConnell said.

"So do I," Pike said.

"Good," McConnell said, standing up, "let's go."

"After the baths."

"Again with the baths," McConnell said, sitting back down.

"If we're going to go to a restaurant and get served," Pike said, "I think it's a good idea."

"Okay, okay," McConnell said, standing up again, "let's get it over with."

17

"You have some clean clothes in that sack?" Pike asked his friend.

"Of course I do," McConnell said. "A clean shirt, anyway."

"I guess that'll do for now," Pike said. "Let's go down the hall and see if those bathtubs are filled yet."

Pike and McConnell walked down the hall with their fresh clothes and found the bathtubs in a room at the end. From the steam that was rising from the tubs, the water was pretty hot. There were also towels set aside for them.

They undressed and Pike settled himself into the tub. McConnell, still reluctant, took a few minutes to finally immerse himself in the water.

"Is that so bad?" Pike asked.

"Actually," McConnell said, "the heat feels kind of nice. Soothing, you know?"

"I know."

They were only in the tubs about three minutes when the door opened and two men entered. From the looks on their faces, they were not happy to find the tubs occupied.

"What the hell do ya think you're doin'?" one of them asked. He was a large man with broad shouders and a lantern jaw. His friend was not as tall, but he matched his friend in width, and temper.

"Those are our baths," the second man bellowed.

"Well, if that's true," Pike said, "we're sorry we took them, but as we're already wet, we might as well finish up. You can get two fresh tubs when we're done."

"We don't want fresh tubs," the first man said, "we want these."

Pike looked over at McConnell, who shrugged.

"I'm finished, Pike," McConnell said, "if these fellas

18

want these tubs, it's all right with me."

Pike concurred with his friend and they both stood up and stepped from the tubs, reaching for their towels.

"Don't touch them towels," the first man said. "You'll get them wet."

"That's the idea, friend," Pike said. "The towels get wet and we get dry. We'll have fresh towels sent up for you."

"We don't want fresh towels," the second man said, "we want them towels."

Pike took a good look at the men now and they didn't seem to be ready for baths, either of them. They weren't well dressed, but their clothes were clean and they each had a large knife on their belts. Pike's knife, and Kentucky pistol, were back in his room, as were McConnell's.

"Get movin'," Lantern Jaw said.

Suddenly, Pike realized that what these men were really looking for was a fight—what he didn't know was whether they just wanted a fight with anyone, or with him and McConnell in particular.

"Look," McConnell said, "we are not walking down the hall dripping wet."

"You're either walking down the hall," the second man said, "or you're flying down it."

"That's enough of this," Pike said. "If you two are looking for a fight, look somewhere else."

"I don't think so," Lantern Jaw said, pulling his knife. "I think we found one we like right here."

Pike looked at McConnell, and then down at one of the tubs. As the second man produced his knife, Pike grasped one end of the tub and McConnell the other. Muscles bulged as they lifted and then emptied it on the two intruders.

The water was still sufficiently hot for the men to shout, fearing that they'd be burned. They dropped their knives and Pike and McConnell moved in.

Naked, the two mountain men made quick work of the drenched men. Pike punched Lantern Jaw in the throat, and when the man fell to the floor, choking, Pike laid the empty tub over his head.

McConnell hit the other man in the stomach, then grabbed his arm and swung him toward the second tub. The man went head first into the water, tipping the tub over. The man sprawled to the floor, spitting out water.

Pike looked at McConnell and said, "Well, they got baths whether they wanted them or not."

Still naked, carrying their towels and clothes, the two mountain men walked back down the hall to their room. As they reached their door, another door opened and a woman stepped out. She was tall, red-haired, pale-skinned and beautiful. She stopped short when she saw the two naked men, then smiled and boldly studied them, with special attention paid to Pike.

"Uh," Pike said, embarrassed, "you'll have to excuse us—"

"For what?" she asked. "I've finally started a day out right."

With that she turned and walked toward the stairs, hips twitching interestingly beneath her dress. Both men felt themselves reacting, and Pike said, "We'd better get inside and get dressed before somebody sets the law on us."

Pike entered the room and, with a last look at the retreating back of the red-haired woman, McConnell followed.

After Pike and McConnell had dried off and finished dressing, they went down to the lobby to ask the clerk for a decent place to eat. Pike made sure he had his knife on, and his Kentucky pistol tucked into the front of his pants.

"There's a cafe just down the street, if all you're interested in is meat and potatoes," the clerk told them. "It's nothing fancy."

"We're not looking for anything fancy," Pike said. "Thanks."

"Uh, excuse me," the clerk said.

"Yeah?" McConnell asked.

"Uh, would you gentlemen know anything about a flood on your floor?"

"Not us," Pike said, exchanging glances with McConnell, "but there should be two fellas coming down in a few minutes who are soaking wet—clothes and all. You might want to ask them about it."

They left the clerk with a puzzled look on his face, and water leaking onto his desk from the ceiling.

CHAPTER TWO

Over their meal, Pike put the question he'd been thinking about to McConnell.

"You think those guys came looking for us?" McConnell asked.

"It's a thought," Pike said. "They sure weren't looking for a bath, were they?"

"Now that you mention it, no," McConnell said, "but maybe they were just looking for a fight . . . with anyone."

"That's a possibility, too," Pike said.

"All right," McConnell said, "if they were looking for us, why?"

"Maybe they were sent."

"By who?"

Pike shrugged.

"Maybe by the people we came to see."

"The fur companies?" McConnell said. "Which one?"

"That's something we'll have to find out."

"How did they know we were here?"

"Maybe one of their representatives got them a message."

"I guess we should have asked those two jaspers

some questions, huh?"

"Maybe we'll still get the chance," Pike said. "They sure ain't gonna be happy about what happened."

"You figure they'll try again?"

"Wouldn't you? Whoever hired them ain't gonna be too happy, either."

"So all we have to do is wait for them to try again, and then find out who sent them."

"Or we can ask the companies direct."

"Sounds all right to me," McConnell said. "So when are we gonna do that?"

Pike looked at his empty plate, and at McConnell's, and said, "How about now?"

They grabbed a buggy in front of the hotel and Pike gave the driver the address of the Hudson Bay Company. Both Pike and McConnell studied the crowded streets dubiously, not eager to get out of the buggy and join the flow of foot traffic.

"In the mountains," McConnell said, "we don't see this many people in a year."

Pike indicated two lovely women who were walking down the street, one fair-haired, the other dark, but both with pale skin.

"We don't see too many women like that in the mountains, either."

"You got that right," McConnell had to admit, eyeing the two women.

The buggy pulled up in front of the address they wanted and they got out.

"You want me to go in with you?" McConnell asked.

"No," Pike said, "we don't want it to look like we're ganging up on them. I'm the chosen representative, I'll go up and talk to them."

McConnell looked around, a lost expression on his

face, and Pike spotted a tavern across the street.

"Why don't you go over there and wait for me," he said, pointing.

McConnell looked across the street and said, "Yeah, I could use a drink, or two."

"Don't get too far ahead of me," Pike said. "I'll join you after I'm done here."

"I'll drink real slow," McConnell said.

"Drink beer," Pike suggested, "not whiskey."

"You sayin' I can't handle my whiskey?"

"Would I say that about you, Skins?" Pike asked. "Remember, you and I have tipped glasses together many times."

"Hmmm," McConnell said, remembering many fights they'd gotten into along the way—usually after drinking whiskey.

"I'll have a beer and wait for you," McConnell said.

"Good," Pike said. "See you in a little while."

McConnell entered the tavern and stopped just inside the door. He could smell the wood and leather, nothing like the smells of the makeshift bars he frequented in the mountains. He attracted a lot of attention as he entered, because he didn't fit in. His clothing, his size made him stand out. Many of the men drinking in the place were businessmen who worked in the area, who had stopped in for lunch, or simply for a midday drink. Skins McConnell certainly did not look like a businessman.

McConnell's first instinct was to leave, because he also knew that he didn't fit in, but his thirst made him stay. He approached the bar and waited for the bartender, who noticed him.

"What can I get you?" the bartender asked.

"A beer," McConnell said. "A cold one."

"You think we make a living here selling warm

beer?" the man asked.

"No," McConnell said.

"Then I'll bring you a beer," the bartender said. "It'll be cold, friend."

"Sure," McConnell said. It might have been his imagination, because of what had happened earlier, but it seemed to him the bartender was a bit peckish—as if he were looking for an argument.

When the man brought his beer he thanked him and sipped it.

"Nice and cold," McConnell said, trying to be amiable.

"You ain't from around here, are you?" the bartender asked.

"Uh, no, I ain't."

"That's obvious," the man said. He gave McConnell a distasteful once-over, and then went to the other end of the bar.

The man was shorter and lighter than McConnell, and the mountain man could have easily pulled him across the bar and broken his back, but he decided against it. He was in a strange bar in a strange town, and he decided it would serve him better to keep his instincts in check.

Besides, he couldn't take the whole place on by himself, even though he was starting to get annoyed at being stared at.

He'd wait for Pike.

Two men sitting at a corner table were watching Skins McConnell with more than just a passing interest. Both were dressed in dark suits, like any other businessmen, but their business was not the same as others.

Their business was killing people.

"What do you think?" Robert Cole asked.

"He's perfect," the second man, Leonard Roberts, replied.

Cole was a tall, youthful-looking man with dark hair and a smooth face. Roberts was gray-haired, handsome in a rough way, seemingly the older of the two, which he was, by some fifteen years or so.

For years Len Roberts had plied his trade alone. Over the years he had killed many men, from New York to San Francisco with many stops in between. Two years ago, when he turned fifty, he decided to take on a student. Bob Cole was that student, although by now he was more partner than anything else. Still, Cole was always learning from Roberts, as he was now.

"He's obviously a stranger."

"Also, he doesn't appear to be too bright," Robert Cole said.

"We might even go so far as to assume that," Roberts said, "but let's not count on it."

"Okay. How do we play it, then?"

"We play it easy," Roberts said. "We don't want to spook him. Leave by the back door and get Karen."

"Karen?"

"Yeah," Roberts said. "If I'm any judge, this man needs a woman almost as badly as he needs a beer."

"Where the hell is he from?" Cole asked, studying McConnell again.

"The mountains, lad," Roberts said, "the man is down from the mountains."

When Pike left the building that housed the offices of Hudson Bay, he was shaking his head. He had spent a good twenty minutes talking to Steve Stilwell, the president of the company, but to no avail. The man claimed that the price decrease was necessary to the survival of Hudson Bay. Pike had asked how well

Hudson Bay would survive without the mountain men, but Stilwell had simply shrugged and stated that if it came to that, they'd have to try.

Pike was worried. The Hudson Bay representatives were always among the better liked and most understanding. He'd expected to find that to be the case at the top level of the company, but obviously he was wrong.

He hoped to have better luck elsewhere.

He crossed the street and entered the tavern he and McConnell had agreed to meet at. As he looked around it was obvious that his friend wasn't there.

He ignored the curious eyes that were studying him and walked to the bar, where he ordered a beer. When the man brought it he asked about McConnell.

"I'm looking for a friend," he said.

"We don't do that here, pal," the bartender said.

"Do what?"

"Supply friends," the man said. "Maybe your hotel clerk can help you out if it's a lady you're looking for—"

"No, no," Pike said, "I'm looking for a friend of mine who was supposed to meet me here."

"Oh?"

"Yes, he was dressed a lot like me, so I'm sure you couldn't have missed him."

"Oh, him," the bartender said.

"Then he was here?"

"Oh, sure," the bartender said. "Came in about half an hour ago."

"Do you know where he is now?"

"Nope," the man said. "He left about ten minutes ago."

"Left? But he was supposed to meet me here."

"I guess he got a better offer."

"What's that mean?"

"It means your friend left with a lady."

"I thought you didn't do that here."

"We don't," the man said. "If she was a whore she was on her own. Maybe she was just a lady looking for a friend. Your friend didn't seem to have to be forced to leave."

"Was she attractive?"

"Mister," the man said, "she was the best-looking thing to walk in here in a month of Sundays. That's why . . ."

"That's why what?"

"Uh, that's why I was, uh, surprised that she picked your friend . . . uh, no offense meant."

"None taken."

"Any more questions?"

"No," Pike said. "I'll just drink my beer and wait. He'll come back when he's finished."

"If it was me," the man said, wiggling his eyebrows, "I wouldn't be finished for a long time."

"If it's that long," Pike said, "I'll ask for another beer."

"Second one's on the house," the bartender said. "Just wave if you want it."

"Thanks."

"Sure."

Pike looked around and didn't see any open tables. Half the people there had gone back to what they were doing, while the other half were still looking him over. Surely he couldn't be the only man of his size that they had ever seen in St. Louis.

Could he?

CHAPTER THREE

After two hours Pike started to worry.

It wasn't unlike Skins McConnell to go off with a good-looking woman at a moment's notice, but it was unlike him to leave Pike waiting for so long.

Something had to be wrong.

Pike went back to the bar.

"Ready for that second beer?" the man asked.

"Sure."

The bartender drew him another beer and put it on the bar in front of him. Pike left it standing there.

"Looks like your friend must be having a good time," the man said.

"Do you know the woman he left with?"

"Thought I mentioned that before," the man said. "I never saw her before she walked in here. I'd remember."

"What did she do when she walked in?"

"Huh? Whataya mean?"

"Did she sit at a table? Did my friend approach her? What was the first thing she did when she walked in?"

"Well," he said, scratching his head, "I noticed her right away. She came in the front door, looked around, then looked over at the bar and walked up to your friend."

"She never sat down?"

"No."

"She went right to my friend?"

"Well . . ."

"Well what?"

"It was a funny thing," the bartender said.

"What was?"

"Well, for a minute I thought she saw somebody she knew."

"Where?"

"In the back," the bartender said. "She looked back there for a few moments, then I thought she nodded. I expected her to walk back there, but instead she walked over to the bar and engaged your friend in conversation."

"Do you recall who she was looking at when she nodded?" Pike asked.

"Sorry, friend," the man said. "There were a lot of men in here."

"You said she looked in the back. Where, exactly?"

"At that table in the corner."

Pike looked over at the table, then walked over to it. He walked around it, looked under it, and then walked back to the bar.

"You don't remember who was sitting there?"

"Best I can recollect, two men."

"Were they still there when I came in?"

The man scratched his head again.

"Now that you mention it, no, they weren't," he said.

"When did they leave?"

"Seems to me they left right after your friend left with the woman."

"And you can't remember who they were?"

"Best I can tell you, friend, is if I had known them, I'd remember," the man said, apologetically. "They must have been strangers to me."

"How were they dressed?"

"Is there some kind of trouble—"

"Silly question," Pike said. "How were they dressed?"

"Well, they must have been dressed like everyone else, or I would have noticed—like you and your friend. I noticed the two of you right off because you're dressed different. They must have been wearing suits."

"Like the other men in this room now?"

The bartender looked around and said, "Yeah, like businessmen. Hey, what's going on?"

"My friend seems to be missing," Pike said.

"Just 'cause he went off with a woman?"

"He wouldn't have left me here waiting this long."

"Mister," the bartender said, "you didn't see this woman."

"No, I didn't."

"Why don't you go to the police?"

"Maybe I will," Pike said, "after I check our hotel."

Pike turned to leave and the man said, "Hey, don't you want your second beer?"

"I'll come back for it."

"I hope you find your friend!" the bartender called as Pike left.

Pike hoped so, too.

Pike went back to the hotel. Not only was McConnell not in their room, but there was no sign that he was ever there since they had left earlier. Nevertheless he checked with the clerk, who confirmed it.

"I haven't seen your friend since the both of you left here earlier," he said.

"Thanks. Where is the nearest police station?"

"You can walk," the clerk said, and gave him directions. It was a four-block walk.

Pike had never been in a police station before. In fact, he had rarely seen a lawman. Usually, in the mountains, he and his fellow mountain men made their own law.

He entered the police station and saw a huge wooden desk with a uniformed man sitting behind it.

"Can I help you?" the policeman asked.

"I hope so," Pike said. "My friend is missing."

"Whataya mean, missing?"

"Just that," Pike said. "I can't find him."

"If you can't find him, that don't necessarily make him missing."

"What would you call it?"

"Tell me what happened?"

Pike gave the man the short version, starting with their arrival.

"You think these other two fellas found him?"

"It's a possibility," Pike said.

"The bartender said he left with a girl, though."

"She might have been working with them."

"Maybe you'd better talk to somebody."

"Isn't that what I've been doing?" Pike said. "You're the law, ain't you?"

"I just write this stuff down, friend," the policeman said. "You'll have to talk to Inspector Emerson."

"Who's Inspector Emerson?"

"Just have a seat and I'll get him out here."

Pike looked around, saw a long wooden bench, and sat on it. He wondered if the law always worked at this pace in the city.

After the policeman returned to the desk Pike waited another ten minutes before a second man appeared. He was wearing a dark suit and a boiled white shirt. He was tall and slender, sandy-haired, in his late thirties or early forties.

"Mr. Pike?" he asked, approaching the bench.

"That's right," Pike said, standing.

"I'm Inspector Earl Emerson."

Emerson was tall, but Pike towered over him.

"I understand you have a problem."

"That's right."

"Why don't you tell me about it?"

"I just finished telling him about it," Pike said, indicating the policeman behind the desk.

"Well, suppose you tell it to me, again."

Pike hesitated a moment, then told the same story to Emerson.

"What does your friend look like?" Emerson asked. The look on his face, and the tone of his voice, told Pike it was not just an idle question."

"Why?"

"Just describe him."

Pike did so, in detail.

"Come with me."

"Where?"

"Just follow me."

Emerson turned to walk away, but Pike grabbed his arm and turned him back around.

"I want to know what's going on."

"Give me a minute and you'll see," Emerson said. "Come with me?"

Pike removed his hand from the inspector's arm and said, "Lead the way."

The inspector led Pike down a long hallway to a flight of steps that led down. At the bottom of the stairs they came to a barred door, with a guard on the other side.

"Open up," Emerson said.

The guard opened the door.

"Give him your pistol," Emerson said, and Pike obliged. The guard let both of them through. Emerson continued down a hall to another barred door, which was also opened to them by an armed guard.

"What the hell—" Pike said.

"This way."

Emerson led Pike along a row of cells until they finally stopped in front of one.

Pike looked inside the cell and saw a man lying on a cot with his back to them.

"Skins?"

The man lifted his head, then turned and looked behind him.

"Pike?"

Pike's relief at finding his friend alive and well turned to anger as he turned to Emerson and said, "What the hell is he doing in there?"

"Then this is your friend?"

"It is," Pike said. "What's he in here for?"

"Pike," McConnell said, "I don't know what's going on, but they put me in here for murder."

"For what?" Pike said. He turned to Emerson and said, "Is this some kind of a joke you play on visitors to your city?"

"This is no joke, Mr. Pike," Inspector Earl Emerson said. "Mr. McConnell has been arrested for murder."

CHAPTER FOUR

Pike wanted to talk to McConnell, but Emerson insisted that he first accompany him to his office.

"Who is he supposed to have murdered?"

"A woman named Jennifer Welles."

"Who is she?"

"Mrs. Richard Welles?"

The way Emerson said the name, Pike guessed that he was supposed to recognize it.

"I don't know who that is?"

"Mr. Welles is very probably the next governor of this state."

"Well, good for him. What makes you think my friend killed his wife?"

Emerson hesitated a moment, then said, "He was found lying next to her."

"Where?"

"In a hotel."

"What are you trying to tell me?"

Emerson made a face and said, "This is not to leave this office, Pike."

"All right."

"I mean it. You might think that leaking this to the newspapers would get your friend off. Believe me, it won't. If you do leak this—"

"I won't say a word."

"Do I have your word?"

Pike figured he couldn't help McConnell if he didn't know the whole story.

"They were in bed together."

"McConnell and Mrs. Welles?"

Emerson nodded.

"Apparently, Mrs. Welles liked to slip out from time to time and . . . go to hotels with strange men. One of those men finally killed her."

"Not Skins McConnell."

"We found him lying in bed with her."

"And she was dead?"

"Yes."

"And what was he doing?"

"Sleeping."

"Next to a dead woman?"

"That's right."

"Doesn't that strike you as a little odd?"

"I don't know your friend," Emerson said. "Maybe that was part of the excitement for him."

"Believe me, Inspector," Pike said, "my friend does not get excited by sleeping in bed with dead women, only live ones."

"Well, she was alive when they started."

"I don't believe this," Pike said. "I want to talk to McConnell and get his side."

"His side," Emerson said, "is that he doesn't remember anything."

"I'd like to hear it from him . . . if I may."

Emerson tapped his fingers on the desk top for a few moments, then said, "All right. I'll let you talk to him— in his cell."

"That's fine," Pike said.

"Come with me."

36

Once again Pike followed Emerson down the stairs and through the two sets of cell doors.

"What happens now?" Pike asked on the way. "I'm not familiar with the way the law works in the city."

"How does it work in the mountains?"

"We make our own law, for the most part. There's not often a lawman around when we need one."

"Well, he'll be charged, and a court date will be set for him to stand trial."

"How long will that take?"

"He'll probably be tried within the next two weeks," Emerson said. "If the victim wasn't Mrs. Richard Welles . . ." Emerson trailed off, apparently deciding not to finish that sentence.

"If she wasn't married to an important man it would take longer?"

"Yes," Emerson said. "Considering who her husband is, it might not even take that long."

"Does he have to spend all that time in jail?"

"That will be up to the judge."

"When will he see the judge?"

"Tomorrow."

"Can I be there?"

"Sure," Emerson said. "In the morning, at ten."

"I'll be there."

When they reached McConnell's cell Pike said, "I want to go inside."

"I can't—" Emerson said.

"For Chrissake, he's my friend," Pike said. "He's not going to try to kill me, and I'm not going to try to break him out."

Emerson thought a moment, then said, "All right." Pike had already surrendered his pistol to the first guard, so Emerson unlocked the cell door and let him enter.

"Five minutes," he said.

"Have a heart, Inspector," Pike said.

"All right," the man said, grudgingly, "ten."

Emerson closed the door, locked it and walked away.

"He's all heart, isn't he?" McConnell asked.

He stood up from his cot and the two friends clasped hands, and then hugged.

"What the hell have you gotten yourself into?" Pike demanded. "Can't I leave you alone for five minutes?"

"Sorry," McConnell said.

"Tell me what happened?"

McConnell told his story. He had gone to the tavern to have a beer and wait for Pike, as planned.

"When I walked in they looked at me like I was some sort of animal," he said. "I was gonna leave, but then I figured to hell with them and ordered a beer."

"Did you sit at a table?"

"No, I stood at the bar."

"And then what?"

"Well, I was there about ten minutes when this woman sidles up to me at the bar. Pike, I tell you, she was a vision, this one—"

"Never mind that," Pike said. "Let's just say she aroused your interest."

"That ain't all she aroused," McConnell said. "She asked me to buy her a drink. I said okay, but she said not there."

"Where?"

"She said she had rooms nearby."

"Oh, sure."

"Pike—"

"I know," Pike said, "she was a vision."

"We left together and started walking down the street. She had her arm through mine, her head on my shoulder. I tell you, her perfume—"

"Then what happened?"

McConnell shrugged and said, "I don't know. The next thing I knew I was being shook awake by the law. I was in bed with a dead woman next to me."

"Was the dead woman the woman from the tavern?"

"For a moment I thought so, but then I took a closer look. They're the same type, but it wasn't her."

"Did the first woman give you her name?"

"She said her name was Karen."

"No last name?"

"No."

"It's not going to be easy to find her."

"Let me describe her," McConnell said. "That'll narrow it down."

"All right," Pike said.

McConnell described Karen as medium height, with full lips, big brown eyes, long auburn hair and a full, womanly figure.

"All right," Pike said, "now answer some questions for me."

"Go ahead."

"Did anyone in the tavern take an unusual interest in you when you entered?"

"Sure, everyone."

"I mean beyond the initial interest of a stranger entering the place," Pike said. "Were there two fellas at a back table eyeing you?"

"Not that I noticed."

"Well, were you and Karen followed when you left the tavern?"

Again McConnell said, "Not that I noticed."

Pike rubbed his jaw.

"What do you know?" McConnell said. "Did you talk to the bartender?"

"Yeah, he said you left with a lady, but he also said that there were two men at a back table . . ." He explained how the bartender thought that Karen might

39

have known two men in the place.

"You think the two men put her up to this, and then followed us?"

"It's possible."

"Then they killed this woman and they're trying to put the blame on me."

"That's the only way I can figure it," Pike said, "unless you killed her."

"Jack!"

"Relax, I know you didn't kill her."

"I don't even know who she was?"

"That's the worst part," Pike said, and told McConnell who the woman was.

"That's great," McConnell said, "they'll hang me in the morning."

"It doesn't work that way in the city," Pike said, and explained what Emerson had told him about facing a judge, and then standing trial.

"When do I see the judge?"

"In the morning."

"And then I can get out of here?"

"That'll be up to him."

"You mean I might have to stay in here until the trial?"

"It looks that way."

"How long will that be?"

"Well, that's the only good part about who she was. Since her husband is so important, they might want to start the trial early."

"That's good?"

"In a way," Pike said. "At least you won't have to spend weeks in here—but it also might work against us."

"How?"

"I'm going to need time to find out who really did kill Mrs. Richard Welles."

"How are you gonna do that?"

"I don't know, Skins," Pike said, "but it's the only way I'm going to get you off this hook you're on."

"Oh Christ!" McConnell said, sitting down heavily on the cot. "What a fix I got myself into this time. If I get out of this I'll never look at another woman as long as I live."

"Don't make promises you can't keep, my friend," Pike said.

"Pike," McConnell said, looking up at his friend, "you got to get me out of here."

Pike and McConnell had been through a lot together—Indians, wild animals, the lot—but Pike had never seen his friend this frightened before. Pike didn't blame him. They were in a strange place with no friends to fall back on. All McConnell had was Pike—and that frightened Pike more than a little.

They had saved each other's lives ten times over, but now his friend's life was in his hands in a way it had never been before.

He put his hand on McConnell's shoulder and said, "I'll do my best, Skins."

"Pike?" Inspector Emerson said. "Time's up."

"Not yet, it's not," Pike said to no one in particular. "Not by a long sight."

They went back to Emerson's office.

"I'll need to know where Richard Welles lives."

"What for?" Emerson asked.

"I have to talk to him."

"Pike—"

"Emerson, if that was your friend down there, what would you do?"

"You're not a policeman," Emerson said, "and you're not a detective."

"All of that's true," Pike said. "Unfortunately, once the morning newspaper comes out with the story I'll be the only man in St. Louis who doesn't think that Skins McConnell is a killer. The only way I can prove he's not is to find out who is."

"And how do you intend to do that?"

"I don't know," Pike said, "but it seems to me talking to the victim's husband would be a good start. Husbands have been known to kill wives, even in the mountains."

Emerson stood up and pointed his right index finger at Pike.

"I won't have you harassing an important man like Richard Welles."

"I'm not going to harass him," Pike said. "I'm going to ask him some questions. If he doesn't want to answer them, he doesn't have to."

"That's true," Emerson said, somewhat mollified. "If he doesn't you'll leave him be?"

"Hey," Pike said, innocently, "if he doesn't want to talk to me, what can I do?"

Emerson stood there studying the innocent look on Pike's face. Pike hoped that the man could not see what was going on behind his face. If Welles wouldn't talk to him, he'd pick the man up by the neck and shake him until he would.

"All right," Emerson said, "I'll tell you where he lives. It's a matter of public record, anyway—but if I find you were harassing him—"

"Don't worry, Inspector," Pike said. "I'm a visitor in your city."

Emerson frowned, as if he didn't know exactly what that statement was supposed to mean.

Pike didn't know what it meant, either.

It was just something to say.

Bob Cole was standing at the window of the hotel

room he shared with Leonard Roberts, looking down at the street below.

"Do you think it will stick?" he asked.

Roberts was sitting on one of the beds, dealing himself a game of solitaire.

"It should," he said, without looking up.

"What if it doesn't?"

Now Roberts looked up, frowning.

"What are you worrying about?" he asked his younger partner. "It went off without a hitch, didn't it?"

"Yeah, it did."

"So relax."

"What about Karen?"

"What about her?"

"She knows what we did."

"Karen won't talk, Bob. What the hell's the matter with you?"

"Nothing. When do we get paid?"

"We'll collect tomorrow, after it hits the newspapers," Roberts said, looking back down at his cards.

"Can I come along?"

"Sure," Roberts said, looking up. "You earned it. You killed her, didn't you?"

"Yep," Bob Cole said, "I killed her."

"Yeah, you killed her," Roberts said, grinning.

"Are you all right?" Roberts asked.

"Of course I'm all right," Cole said. "Black jack on red queen."

"I see it."

CHAPTER FIVE

Pike went back to his hotel. When he got there he wondered if he had done all he could do for McConnell. Instead of going to his room he went to the hotel bar. It was almost eight p.m. and he realized that he was hungry. After a beer he'd go and find something to eat.

He ordered the beer from the bartender, a big, burly man who would have fit right in at a rendezvous. He looked like he could wrestle bears.

"Thanks," Pike said. "You ever do any wrestling?"

"Sure," the man said, "and boxing. My nose didn't get like this by itself."

The man's nose was almost flat against his face. His neck and shoulders were thick, his biceps pressed against his shirt like boulders, as if he couldn't get sleeves that fit well. He was not as tall as Pike, but he was wider. His hair was black, cut short and peppered with gray.

"What about you?"

"Some," Pike said.

"Where you from? Not the city."

"No," Pike said, "the mountains."

"A mountain man?"

44

"Yeah," Pike said, "yeah, I'm a mountain man."

"You know," the man said, leaning his elbows on the bar, "I've often thought about going to the mountains."

"You'd like it."

"You think so?"

"Unless you like crowded rooms and streets."

The man looked around the bar, which was half full, and said, "This ain't crowded."

Pike looked around and said, "It is to me."

"Really? This looks crowded to you?"

"In the mountains," Pike said, "you can go a month without seeing this many people, let alone in one place."

"You know, maybe I would like it?" the man said. He stuck his hand out and said, "My name's Joe Pitch."

"Pike." The man's hand was large, heavier than Pike's though not as long. The two men clasped hands briefly, neither feeling the need to participate in a test of strength.

"What are ya doin' in town?"

"We came to talk to the fur companies about lowering the prices they're paying for furs," Pike said. "The visit's turned into something else, though."

"We?"

"Yeah, I came with a friend."

"He in trouble?"

"How'd you know that?"

The man shrugged.

"You're here alone, drinkin' alone, lookin' like you got a problem."

"I do."

"That's what I'm here for," Joe Pitch said. "To listen."

Pike thought about it for a moment, then decided he might as well talk to someone.

He told Pitch about what had happened to McCon-

45

nell, and the man listened intently.

"You need a lawyer."

"I do?"

"Your friend does," Pitch said. "If he's going to court he needs someone to speak for him."

"He can talk for himself."

"No, I mean someone who knows what he's doing in court. Have you or your friend ever been to court?"

"There's not much call for going to court in the Rockies."

"I guess not," Pitch said. "Take my advice, get him a lawyer."

Pike put down his beer mug and rubbed his jaw.

"I wouldn't even know where to start to find him a lawyer."

"Well," Pitch said, "maybe I can help."

There was a moment's hesitation when Pike thought that maybe Pitch was waiting for some money. He put his hand in his pocket and Pitch stopped him.

"No, I'm not asking for money," the burly bartender said. "I'm just trying to think if I know anybody. You know, a lot of people drink here, but it's not the best place in town. I may know a lawyer, but he won't be one of those rich, smooth-talking kind."

"I don't know any kind," Pike said, "so whatever you can do for me, I'd be much obliged."

"I might be able to connect you with somebody. You're stayin' here, right?"

"Right."

"Come and see me tomorrow afternoon," Pitch said.

"All right."

"And go and see your friend in the morning, early, before he goes to court. Have him tell the judge that he's getting a lawyer, and would like to postpone his court date."

"Will that work?"

"Maybe not," Pitch said. "The judge might set a date anyway, but you should have your lawyer by that time, no matter what happens."

"Okay," Pike said. "Hey, I appreciate this. I'm out of my element, here."

"Do you think your friend did it?"

"No," Pike said, "I know he didn't, and I'm gonna prove it."

"For that you need a detective."

Pike laughed.

"I don't even know how we're going to. pay the lawyer."

"Well, maybe I can help you there, too," Pitch said.

"Why are you so helpful?"

Pitch shrugged.

"Maybe I'll want you to show me the mountains after this."

Pike stuck out his hand and said, "You've got yourself a deal."

Pike went down the street to the cafe where he and McConnell had eaten earlier and had dinner. After that he decided to take a walk.

At that time of night the streets of St. Louis weren't that bad—at least, not as crowded as they were during the day. He walked a few blocks, giving the city a chance to impress him, but it didn't. Some of the people did, women in particular, but he didn't see any way he could ever live there. He didn't like the feel of concrete or cobblestones under his feet. He preferred soft fields, or even the frozen grounds of the mountains. He also preferred bathing in a lake than in a tub. The warm water was fine, but nothing made you feel more alive than bathing in the ice cold water of a running lake, and then stepping out and letting the mountain air dry you.

He was thinking about the mountain air when the first man hit him.

Actually, his assailant was more boy than man, but he was big enough to knock him off balance as he slammed into him from behind, and kept on going.

Pike didn't quite know what was going on, but suddenly there was a second assailant on him and then Pike realized that they were trying to rob him.

Still off balance, he allowed himself to be pushed against a stone wall by the second robber.

"Give me your money."

There was a knife in his face but he looked past it at the face of the man wielding it. He was about twenty, tall but very thin. It would have been child's play to take the knife away from him.

"How bad you want it?" Pike asked.

"What?"

A lock of hair had fallen across the lad's forehead, just missing his eyes, and he flicked it back with a shake of his head. The look in his eyes was one of puzzlement.

"How bad do you want my money?" Pike asked again. "Bad enough to kill me?"

"Mister, you're crazy," the lad said. "I got a knife."

"I know," Pike said. "It's right there in my face. I can't miss it."

Actually, it wasn't much of a knife. Pike noticed that the boy's hand was shaking, so he decided to take the knife away from him. He grabbed the thin wrist and twisted it just hard enough to make the boy let go of the knife. Then he took out his own knife, the blade of which dwarfed the boy's knife, and waved it in front of the would-be robber's face.

"This is a knife, son," Pike said.

"Jesus," the boy said, holding his wrist. "You gonna kill me?"

"Who was the other boy?"

"My brother."

"Older or younger."

"Younger," the boy said. "He's sixteen."

"He's big for sixteen," Pike said. "How old are you?"

"Twenty-one."

Pike stared at the boy, who looked away and said, "Nineteen."

"Where's your brother?"

"He's watching us."

"Call him over."

"So you can kill us both?"

"I'm not gonna kill anybody," Pike said. He put his knife away and said, "Call him over."

Now that he had put his knife away he could see the boy's eyes darting back and forth. He was getting ready to run.

"If you run I'll catch you and break your leg," Pike said.

"You think you could catch me?" the boy said, boldly.

"If I can't," Pike said, touching the pistol in his belt, "I'll shoot you in the leg."

The boy's eyes widened as he looked down at the pistol. It was obvious that he believed Pike's lie.

"Now call your brother over."

The boy turned and waved his arm. Pike saw the other boy step from a darkened doorway and cross the street tentatively.

"What's his name?" Pike asked.

"Charlie."

"And yours?"

"Danny."

"Why'd you want my money?"

"Well, whataya think?" Danny said. "To get something to eat."

"Why didn't you just ask me for some money for a

meal?" Pike asked.

"You kiddin'?" Danny said, snorting derisively. "That would be beggin'."

"Oh, and you're too proud to beg."

Danny gave Pike a stern look.

"We ain't no beggars."

"So you'd rather be thieves?"

"We ain't no beggars."

Finally, Charlie reached their side of the street and stopped, staring at them.

"Come on, Charlie," Pike said. "Come closer. I'm not gonna hurt you."

Charlie moved closer until he was standing next to his brother, question in his eyes for the older boy.

"Whataya want from us, mister?" Danny said. "You gonna take us to the police?"

"Maybe," Pike said. "At least in jail you'd get a meal."

"If you call that eatin'," Charlie said.

Pike looked at the younger boy. He was a couple of inches shorter than his brother, but he weighed about thirty pounds more. Somehow, Pike didn't think he'd been on the street as long as his older brother. He had the same lock of hair that kept falling across his forehead, and he removed it with the same practiced flick of his head.

"No, I'm not gonna take you to the police," Pike said.

"Then let us go," Danny said.

"Not yet."

"Whataya gonna do?" Charlie asked.

"I think," Pike said, looking from one boy to the other, "I'll buy you fellas a meal."

At first the boys didn't believe it, but Pike walked them back to the cafe and took them inside.

"Order whatever you want," he told them.

"What do you want for this, mister?" Danny asked.

"Some conversation," Pike said, "your last name."

"What for?"

"You want to eat?"

The two boys exchanged glances and Pike saw Charlie, the younger one, nod.

"All right," Danny said. "Our last name is Sullivan."

"If you're lying to me—"

"That's our name, mister," Charlie said. "Can we eat now?"

Pike smiled at Charlie and said, "Sure, son," and called the waiter over.

Both boys ordered steak, and potatoes, and vegetables, and rolls.

"Can we have whiskey?" Charlie asked, his eyes shining.

"Milk," Pike said. "You can have milk."

"Cold milk?" Charlie asked.

Pike looked up at the waiter, who smiled and said, "Very cold milk."

"All right," Pike said, "bring it. Bring it all."

They answered Pike's questions, but he really didn't know if they were shining him on or not, in return for the meal.

Both boys ate quickly, wolfing their food down. When they were finished they split yet another steak and drank what seemed like gallons of milk.

Danny told Pike that their parents died when he was ten and Charlie was seven. They were sent to an orphanage, and Charlie was adopted almost immediately. The family who wanted him did not want the older boy, and so they were split up.

"I hated it," Charlie said at that point. "I hated being apart from Danny, and I hated the peole who adopted me."

"What happened?" Pike asked.

51

"They brought Charlie back to the orphanage," Danny said, "because he wasn't happy."

"I didn't do what they told me," Danny said, "so they brought me back."

"That must have made you happy," Pike said. "You were together again."

"No," Danny said. "By that time I had run away. I didn't know that Danny had been brought back."

"When did you find out?"

"I didn't," the older boy said.

"When I was twelve, I ran away, too," Danny said. "They found me and brought me back. When I was fourteen, I ran away again. This time they didn't find me."

"What were you doing all this time?" Pike asked Danny.

"Surviving," Danny said. "Living on the streets."

Pike knew that he could survive alone in the mountains for months, but he wasn't sure he could have survived on the streets of a city like St. Louis, not the way this kid seemed to have survived.

"It ain't hard," Charlie said. "There's others. We help each other."

"And rob people?"

Danny looked up sharply and said, "When things get real bad. We don't like doin' it."

"How did you two get back together?" Pike asked.

"After the second time I ran away I kept looking for Danny," Charlie said. "I finally found him."

"That was a year and a half ago," Danny said. "We been together ever since."

"Taking care of each other," Charlie said.

"That's what brothers should do," Pike said.

"Well, we do," Danny said. He sat back from the table and there wasn't a crumb of food left. Charlie sat back with a smile on his face and rubbed his stomach.

52

"That was the best meal I ate in . . . a long time."

"I'm glad."

"We gotta go," Danny said.

"Where?" Pike asked. "Do you have a place to stay? A place to sleep?"

"We'll make out," Danny said, standing up.

Pike stood up, too, and walked outside with them. It was past ten p.m. now, and the streets were even more deserted. When the city was this way, Pike didn't mind it all that much.

"Let's go, Danny," Charlie said.

"You fellas haven't asked me my name," Pike said.

"It don't matter," Danny said. "We'll probably never see you again, mister."

"You could say thank you."

"For what?" Danny asked.

"For the meal."

"We didn't ask you for it."

"But you took it."

"We gave you what you wanted," Danny reasoned, and Pike couldn't argue with that.

"All right," Pike said. "Good luck."

Charlie started away, but Danny didn't move. Suddenly, he stuck out his hand.

"My knife."

"What?"

"You picked up my knife from the ground," Danny said. "I want it."

"Oh, yeah," Pike said. He took the small knife from his pocket and handed it to Danny. Immediately, Danny reversed it and pointed it at Pike's throat.

"Your money."

Pike laughed, took some money out and handed it to the serious-faced boy.

"That all of it?" Danny asked.

"It's all I'm gonna give you, boy," Pike said. "You'd

53

best not push your luck and be on your way."

"Come on, Danny," Charlie said. "This ain't right. He done right by us."

"We take care of ourselves, Charlie," Danny said. "Remember?"

"I remember."

Danny turned abruptly and walked away. Charlie looked at Pike, said, "Thanks, mister," and followed his brother away.

Pike went back to his hotel and for the first time since meeting the Sullivan brothers, he thought about Skins McConnell.

He undressed and stretched out on the bed. He'd have to get up early tomorrow to go and talk to McConnell and give him the legal advice he'd gotten from a bartender.

McConnell might think he was crazy, but up until now Pike didn't know anyone in St. Louis to ask for help except a bartender.

Joe Pitch seemed to know what he was talking about. Pike wondered if Pitch had always been a bartender.

Maybe he'd ask him, tomorrow.

PART TWO

THE LAWYER AND
THE DETECTIVE

CHAPTER SIX

Pike woke early the next morning and had breakfast in the hotel dining room, which was empty. Pike thought that was because it was so early, but after he tasted the food he realized that wasn't the reason.

After breakfast—most of which he had not eaten—he went directly to the police station and asked to see McConnell.

The policeman at the desk did not know Pike, and when Pike asked for Inspector Emerson, he was told that the inspector was not in.

"When will he be in?"

"He don't report to me," the man on the desk said.

"Look," Pike said, "I was here last night and Inspector Emerson allowed me to see McConnell."

"I can't help that," the policeman said. "You ain't his lawyer, and I don't have the authority to let you in to see him."

"Well, who does?"

"Inspector Emerson."

"And he's not here yet."

The man grinned and said, "Now you're getting the picture, friend."

"Who's in charge right now?"

"Lieutenant Healy."

"Can I see him?"

"Have a seat and I'll see if he's busy."

Pike sat on the same wooden bench as the night before and waited. After about ten minutes a man came out with the policeman from the desk. He was not tall, perhaps five ten. He was in excellent physical condition without being musclebound, or bulky. Youngish looking, the gray in his black hair and mustache stamped him as being in his late thirties, or early forties.

"Are you Pike?"

"That's right."

"I'm Lieutenant Jerry Healy. Inspector Emerson told me about you."

"What did he tell you?"

"That you had a friend who had been arrested for murder, and that you might be by here early this morning."

"Is that all?"

"No," Healy said, "he said that when you arrived I should let you speak to your friend."

"That was real nice of him."

"Yeah," Healy said, "he's real nice. Me, on the other hand, I'm not always so nice."

"Which means what?"

"Which means I don't see why I should let you see McConnell. Not after what he did."

"How am I supposed to react to that?" Pike said. "As far as I know, McConnell's been arrested for murder, but he hasn't been convicted."

"That's only because he hasn't seen a judge yet."

"He's going to need a lawyer."

"A lawyer isn't going to help him."

"I have to talk to him about getting one."

Healy didn't respond.

"He's got the right to one, doesn't he?"

"He does."

"Well, I'm going to pay for it, so I'd like to discuss it with him."

Healy looked up at Pike, who was a half a foot taller than the police lieutenant. Pike decided to wait for the man to make his mind up without pushing him.

"All right, Pike," Healy finally said, "I'll let you see your friend, but only because I want him properly represented when he's sentenced to hang."

"Why do I get the feeling there's something personal in your feelings, Lieutenant?"

Healy's jaw tightened.

"Richard Welles is a friend of mine," Healy said, "and so was his wife."

A thought leaped into Pike's mind. The lieutenant was a good-looking man, and if what he'd heard about Mrs. Welles was true . . . well, he wondered just how friendly Healy and Mrs. Welles really were.

"I want to see your friend get exactly what's coming to him."

"Well then, Lieutenant, that gives us something in common," Pike said, "because I want exactly the same thing."

"I don't think so, Mr. Pike," Healy said. "Not exactly the same thing. Come on, I'll take you down."

"You got all this from a bartender?" Skins McConnell asked.

"I have the feeling he wasn't always a bartender," Pike said.

"What was he, then?"

"Well, he used to be a fight—"

"Great," McConnell said, "we're taking legal advice from a fighting bartender."

59

"The advice makes sense, Skins," Pike said. "You have to admit that."

"Yeah, I guess you're right," McConnell said, dejectedly.

"So you'll do it then," Pike said, "ask the judge to put off your trial until you can get a lawyer?"

"I'll ask," McConnell said. "What harm can that do? What if he gives me a date, though?"

"When that date comes around, we'll have a lawyer there with you."

"A lawyer recommended by the bartender, right?" McConnell said, rolling his eyes.

"Do you know anyone else who'll recommend one?" Pike asked.

"No," McConnell said, "no."

"All right," Pike said, standing up. "Skins, do you remember anything else about yesterday?"

"Not much," McConnell said, rubbing the back of his neck and grimacing.

"What's wrong with your neck?"

"I don't know," he said, pulling his hand away. "It's sore."

"Could you have been hit there?"

"I guess it's possible."

"Maybe we should have a doctor look at you."

"Naw, it's fine."

"We might need to have a doctor say that you were hit," Pike said.

"You think you can get a doctor in here?"

Pike thought a moment, then said, "Not past Lieutenant Healy, but maybe when Inspector Emerson comes in. I'll try asking him later."

"What are you going to do now?"

"I'm going to talk to the husband of the woman you supposedly killed."

*   *   *

Lieutenant Healy was still waiting by the front desk for Pike.

"Well?" he asked.

"Thank you, Lieutenant."

"You better get your friend a real good lawyer, Mr. Pike," Healy said. "He's going to need the best."

"Is there anyone you'd care to recommend, Lieutenant Healy?"

Healy snorted, turned and walked away.

Pike turned and left the police station.

Robert Cole was standing across the street from the police station when Pike exited. He didn't know why, exactly, except that he'd had an urge to leave the hotel room, get away from Leonard Roberts for a little while.

When he first met Roberts, Cole was a thief, sometimes a con man. He had killed two men, and both had been—in his mind—justified. In fact, in the eyes of the law one of them would have been deemed justifiable. He'd been working a con on a wealthy older woman, taking her to bed while taking her for as much of her money as he could. Her husband had burst in on them and had started shooting at them. The bullets the man had fired at Cole hit the man's wife. Cole had time to roll off the bed, grab up his own gun and fire. Husband and wife were both dead. Cole had relieved them both of whatever money they were carrying at the time, which was much less than he had anticipated getting. After that he dressed and hurriedly left the hotel—and the city of Boston in a hurry. He didn't even know what the final outcome of the police investigation had been, and he didn't care.

The second man he killed had been a simple case of intense hatred. The man knew that Cole was a con man and insisted on calling him names like "gigolo," in

61

public. Cole knew he'd never be able to get anything going in Chicago while the man was alive, so one night he sneaked up on him and killed him. He felt that he had done it so ingeniously—waiting until the man was alone, no witnesses, no one even to see him enter and leave the man's building—that he hadn't even bothered to leave Chicago afterward.

A man *had* seen him, however.

Leonard Roberts.

From the moment he met Roberts he became the man's pupil, and then his partner. Roberts had killed a lot of men. Even Cole didn't know how many for sure. Since they'd met five years ago they'd killed sixteen, all of which they had been paid a lot of money for. Lately, they were demanding so much money—and getting it—that they only had to kill two people a year to live comfortably for the past two years.

Mrs. Richard Welles had been their second this year, and it was only May. Somehow, the money they'd gotten for their first job this year was gone. Cole suspected that Roberts had started to gamble, and had even spent a lot of the money on whores. Roberts controlled the money, and he had simply said that their expenses had gone up.

Cole was worried about Roberts. The older man didn't seem satisfied with his life anymore, not the way it had been for the past five years. The gambling and the whores were new this year. Cole was worried; he had to get away and take a walk.

For some reason he found himself in front of the police station where he knew the man they'd framed was being held. He hadn't even realized he was walking that way until he stopped, looked across the street and saw it. When he saw Pike leave he didn't know who he was, but he recognized him as a mountain man. The man they had framed—the newspapers had called him

62

Skins McConnell—was a mountain man, also. How many such men could there be in St. Louis? This one had to have been there to see the other one. They must be friends.

Didn't Karen say something about the man having a partner?

This man would obviously try to help his friend.

Could this be a problem?

He'd have to tell Roberts about this—but maybe he'd follow the man for a while first and see what happened.

As Pike started down the street away from the police station, Cole stepped out of the doorway he'd been standing in and walked across the street, keeping just a little behind the big man.

He wondered where the man was going?

CHAPTER SEVEN

Pike had never seen anything like the home Richard Welles lived in. It was the biggest house he had ever seen, with white columns, three floors, all brick and so many windows! When he first laid eyes on it he thought that surely this could not be one family's home, but then he realized he was in the city, where money was everything, and could buy anything.

That was one of the things he loved about the mountains. You really didn't need a lot of money to live comfortably—and yet even the little money the mountain men made was being cut by the fur companies. That was the real reason Pike was here in St. Louis, yet how could he work on that when Skins McConnell's life was in danger.

He shook his head to dispel thoughts about the fur companies. That would have to come later. Right now he needed to talk to Richard Welles. His only problem was that he didn't know what he would say to the man.

He walked to the front door and knocked. He was conscious of the way he looked, knowing that in these surroundings he would look even worse than usual in his buckskins, but the farthest thing from his mind of late had been buying new clothes.

He would just have to make do.

When the door opened he expected to see Richard Welles. He didn't know what the man looked like, but at least he had expected to see a man, not a beautiful woman.

The woman was tall, full-bodied, with long, luxurious black hair and fair skin. She appeared to be in her early thirties. He removed his hat hurriedly.

"Yes?" she asked, giving Pike a frank appraisal.

"Um, excuse me, ma'am, but is this where Richard Welles lives?"

"It is."

"I'd like to speak to him, please."

"About what?"

"Well . . . it's about his wife's death."

"What have you to do with that?"

"Well, ma'am, I'd really rather explain that to him—" Pike started, but the woman cut him off.

"He's not at home right now," she said, "so I suppose you'll have to explain it to me."

"Can you tell me where he is?"

"I couldn't tell you exactly, no. He's probably out shaking hands and kissing babies." Her tone made it clear that whatever the man was doing, she disapproved. "There is an election coming up, you know . . . or do you know?"

"I'm not from the city, ma'am—"

"Really?" she asked, looking amused.

"—but I do understand that there is an election coming up. I'm just surprised that he would . . ." Pike wasn't sure how to phrase what he was thinking, but the woman saved him the trouble.

"That he would be out on the campaign trail after what happened yesterday? Believe me, Mr. . . ."

"Pike."

"Mr. Pike, believe me when I say my brother will let

nothing stand between him and the election."

"He's your brother, then?"

"Oh, yes," she said, "my big brother. Would you like to come in? Perhaps you can explain things to me over some coffee or tea . . . or something stronger?"

"Thank you," he said, "I'd like that."

He waited for her to step aside to allow him to enter, and when she didn't he tried slipping by her. He could feel the firmness of her body as he pressed against her.

"My, but you're a big one, aren't you?" she asked, holding her ground.

Feeling the need to joke he said, "And I'm the runt of the litter."

She laughed, and he felt as if she had run her fingers up and down his spine.

She closed the door and said, "Come this way, please, Mr. Pike."

"Jack," he said, "my name is Jack."

"I'm Lila Welles, Jack," she said, leading him down a hall and into a room that was lined with books.

She saw the way he was looking around and said, "Haven't you ever seen books before?"

"I've seen a book or two in my time, ma'am—"

"Lila, please."

"Lila . . . but I've never seen this many in one place at one time."

"Yes, well, my brother thinks it helps his image to bring people in here to chat and have them be impressed by his library."

"Has he read all these books?"

"Hardly," she said. "What will you have?"

"Coffee would be fine, ma—uh, Lila, or tea—"

"I'm having something stronger," she said, indicating a small bar with several bottles atop it.

"Well, all right, then," he said. "I'll have what you're having."

66

"Brandy."

"Fine," he said, although he had never tasted brandy before.

She took out two huge, round glasses and poured a small amount of brandy into each. He wondered why she had chosen such large glasses.

She handed him one and he said, "Thank you."

He was waiting for her to take a drink before he did, but she was simply swirling the liquor around in the glass and sniffing it. He did the same. It had a much gentler aroma than whiskey, but it was obviously some sort of liquor.

Finally, she sipped it slowly and he followed, taking a small amount into his mouth.

"You've never had brandy before, have you?" she asked.

"No."

"How is it?"

He looked a bit sheepish and said, "When I drink liquor it's usually something a little harsher."

"I do have whiskey," she said. "Would you prefer some of that?"

"No," he said. "This is fine." He really hadn't gone there to drink, anyway, so it didn't much matter if he enjoyed what he was having.

"Why don't we sit down and you can tell me what connection you have with Jennifer's death."

He sat on one end of a soft sofa and she sat at the other. There was one cushion separating them.

"I really don't have any connection with her death—" he said, and then stopped to formulate his thoughts. He put the brandy glass down on a nearby table.

"Let me make this as simple as possible," he said.

"Please do."

"My partner and I arrived in St. Louis only

yesterday," he said, "and he was arrested last night for killing Mrs. Welles."

"I see," Lila Welles said. "And did he kill my darling sister-in-law?"

"No, ma'am—uh, no, Lila. Fact is, he didn't even know her."

"But he was discovered in bed with her," Lila Welles said, obviously confused.

"He doesn't know how that happened," Pike said. "He was in a tavern waiting for me, and he left with a woman."

"Jennifer?"

"No," Pike said, "although he says that the woman he left with was the same type."

"Could he have left with her, and be mistaken?"

"No," Pike said. "My friend knows how to tell women apart."

"I see," she said. "Is that something you need to know to get along in the mountains?"

"It's something he just knows."

"You mean women?"

"Yes."

"And you?"

"I don't understand."

"Do you know women?"

"I've known a few," he said, not understanding where the conversation was going—or how it got going this way. "In any case, I have to try and prove that he didn't kill your sister-in-law."

"And how do you propose to do that?"

"I'll have to find the man who did."

"I see," Lila said. "Are you a detective?"

"No, I am not," Pike said.

"Then how do you propose to go about this?"

"I don't know," he said, with a shrug. "I'll just have to ask questions."

"I see," she said again, "and you wanted to ask Richard some."

"Yes."

"Like, did he kill his own wife?"

"Well . . ." Pike said. "I wouldn't have asked him that."

"But you're thinking it."

Pike shrugged again.

"I just wanted to talk to him."

"Well, he should be back sometime tonight," she said. "You can check back later."

"Will he talk to me?"

She smiled and said, "Just make him think you're a voter."

Lila Welles stood up, and Pike followed.

"I'll walk you out."

"Thank you."

As they walked to the front door she said, "Is there anything you would like to ask me?"

"I don't think so."

At the door she turned to face him, stopping so abruptly that he bumped into her. Again he was aware of how full and firm her body was.

"Don't you want to know if I killed her?"

"It never occurred to me—"

"I could have, you know," she said, interrupting him. "Jennifer and I aren't—weren't—exactly the best of friends."

"Do you live here with them?"

"No," she said, "I came to be by my brother's side in his time of grief—only the bastard wasn't here when I got here this morning."

Pike frowned. Lila Welles didn't seem to like her brother any more than she had her sister-in-law.

"You're shocked, right?"

"Well . . ."

69

"By my frankness, or my language?"

"Well . . ."

"Women don't talk that way in the mountains?"

"No, they don't."

"Maybe you need to be exposed to a different kind of woman," she said, moving closer to him. He felt his body reacting to her, and he was sure she was the kind of woman who could sense it.

"Maybe," he said. "Uh, I'll come back later this evening and try to catch your brother."

"You do that," she said, putting her hand on his chest and moving her forefinger in a circular motion. "I won't tell him you were here."

"Why not?"

She grinned and said, "He might run away if I do."

"Do you think he killed his wife?"

"Oh," she said, taking her finger from his chest, "I don't think I'd like to answer that question just now." She put her finger on him again and said, "Ask me again when we . . . know each other a little better."

The moment was an awkward one for Pike, and he finally reached for the door and said, "Thanks for your time."

"Sure," she said.

As he opened the door she asked, "What hotel are you staying in?"

Pike had to grope for the name of it and finally said, "The Carlyle."

She wrinkled her nose and said, "Not the best accommodations in town, but there are worse."

"I can't afford the best," he said, "and if I'm here long enough, I may have to find the worst."

"Too bad Jennifer's dead," Lila said. "She could have helped you with that."

"What do you mean?"

Lila smiled, a wide, catty smile, and said, "She's

sampled some of the worst accommodations in town—with some of the worst company."

Pike knew what she was saying. It seemed that the rumors about Jennifer Welles were true, if her sister-in-law knew what she was talking about.

"I always suspected it might get her killed," Lila added. "See you tonight, Jack Pike."

She closed the door on him before he had a chance to say anything else.

Across the street from the Welles house, Robert Cole waited nervously for Pike to come out.

What the hell was the man doing there? It had been a shock to Cole when he realized where the mountain man was going. He fidgeted back and forth from foot to foot until the door finally opened and the man came back out. He'd been inside for almost half an hour.

Cole wondered what he had found out in that time.

Leonard Roberts wondered where Robert Cole was. Cole had left the hotel early that morning, and hadn't yet returned. It was now late afternoon, and Roberts was starting to get antsy.

Although they had been together for five years—pupil and teacher at first, and then partners—Roberts never fully trusted Cole. In point of fact, Roberts never trusted anyone, he just *mis*trusted Cole less than everyone else.

Lately, however, he had caught the younger man looking at him strangely from time to time. Although Roberts was trying to hide the gambling from the younger man, he knew Cole wasn't stupid. Sooner or later his young partner would work up the nerve to call him on it, and at that point Roberts would have to make a decision about what to do with him.

Ever since they had killed the Welles woman, Cole had been looking at him even more often, and with even odder expressions.

Maybe Cole had gone to the police to turn him in—but if he did that he'd be turning himself in, as well.

No, Bob wouldn't do that.

Roberts stood by the window for the next hour, and finally saw Cole coming down the street. He was walking with the short, choppy steps of a man in a hurry who is trying to look like he's not in a hurry.

Roberts went over to the bed and reclined on it, waiting for the door to open. When it did, Cole was in a sweat, a worried look on his face.

"We got problems," Cole said.

"Take it easy," Roberts said, "and tell me about it."

CHAPTER EIGHT

When Pike got back to his hotel he went directly to the bar. When he didn't see Joe Pitch behind the bar he wondered if the bartender had been just talking last night, but then he saw the man sitting at a table. Pitch spotted Pike at the same time and waved him over. By the time Pike reached the table Pitch had attracted the attention of the bartender, who brought over two beers. Pitch downed what was left of the one he'd been working on, and the bartender took the empty away with him.

"I thought you weren't here," Pike said.

"I'm not working today, but I wanted to make sure I was here when you got here. I don't want you thinkin' I talk through my hat."

"What?"

"I want you to know I mean what I say," Pitch said. "I have a lawyer for you."

"That's great. Where is he?"

"He'll be here in about an hour, but I gotta warn you, he ain't got the best reputation."

"What kind of reputation does he have?"

"Dirty," Pitch said. "By that I mean he's a dirty fighter. If this thing gets down in the dirt and the mud,

73

he's your best bet."

"He sounds fine to me," Pike said. "What's his name?"

"Dundee, Andy Dundee," Pitch said. "He's a runt of a guy with a mean temper in court. He don't like judges, and he don't like prosecutors, and he's not on very good terms with the police."

"Otherwise," Pike said, "he's just perfect."

"You decide when you meet him," Pitch said. "Meanwhile, while we wait, tell me about these mountains of yours . . ."

Pike talked, and they went through two more beers before Pitch lifted his head and said, "There he is."

Pike turned and got his first look at Andy Dundee. He was about five five, and if he weighed one hundred and forty pounds, it was when he was soaking wet. He was wearing a suit of clothes that hung on him. His lean jaw was dark with beard stubble, and he had a black patch over his left eye.

"Is the patch real?" Pike asked.

"He's always got a different story for it," Pitch said, "but the eye's gone, all right."

Pitch waved and Dundee spotted them and walked over. On the way he bumped into a larger man, spilling some of the beer the man was carrying.

"Hey, you—" the larger man started, but Dundee fixed him with a cold, one-eyed stare and the man shut his mouth and moved on.

"He's a mean little bugger," Pitch said. "Did I tell you that?"

"Not in those words, no."

"Hello, Joe," Dundee said. "This the guy?"

"Jack Pike, meet Andy Dundee."

Pike started to get up and Dundee put a hand on his

shoulder. Pike was surprised at the strength in the man's hand.

"Don't stand up, Pike," Dundee said, "or we'll start off on the wrong foot. I know I'm short, I don't need it rubbed in." He turned his single brown eye on Pitch and said, "Can a guy get a beer around here?"

Pitch raised his hand and the bartender brought over three fresh beers.

"I understand you need a lawyer," Dundee said after downing half the beer impressively.

"My friend does," Pike said.

"Well, you got one."

"Don't you want to hear—"

"He's been arrested for the murder of Jennifer Welles, right?"

Pike looked at Pitch, who said, "I didn't tell him."

Dundee looked at Pike and said, "I may have one eye, but I can still read a newspaper. A mountain man gets arrested for killing the wife of a prominent St. Louis resident, and another mountain man goes looking for a lawyer."

"You make it sound simple."

"It ain't, believe me," Dundee said. "And this case ain't gonna be easy—and don't worry about my 'ain'ts,' I don't use 'em in court."

Pike hadn't even noticed Andy Dundee's "ain'ts."

"Do you know who Richard Welles is?" Dundee asked.

"Yes."

"No," Dundee said, "you only think you do. I'll tell you who Welles is. He's the sonofabitch who is gonna sell this city down the river to get into the governor's mansion, and from there he thinks he's goin' to the White House. Well, he ain't."

"He's not?"

"I'm gonna stop the sonofabitch, and I'm gonna use

this case to do it."

"How are you gonna do that?" Pike asked.

Dundee frowned at Pike and said, "You don't talk like a mountain man."

"I'm originally from the east."

"Where?"

"I don't talk about that."

"Been back there?"

"Not for years."

"This city stuff must be a shock to your system."

"It is."

"And your friend? McConnell?"

"Him, too."

"And this ain't makin' it much easier, huh?"

"No, it's not," Pike said. "Why do you want to stop Welles?"

"Because he's out for himself and nobody else. I've got no use for so-called public servants who are out for themselves."

"How is this case going to help you?"

"One of two ways," Dundee said. "When I prove that your friend didn't kill Jennifer Welles, maybe I can prove that her husband did."

"What if he didn't?"

"Why should that worry you?" Dundee asked. "You want your friend to get off, right?"

"Not at the expense of an innocent man," Pike said. "If Welles did it, fine, but if he didn't—"

"All right," Dundee said. "So you got scruples. I can live with 'em—yours, I mean. I don't have any, myself."

"You talked about two ways."

"Yeah, the second way is that in proving your friend innocent, I can at least smear Welles all over the newspapers."

"Won't publicity help him?"

Dundee smiled wolfishly and said, "Not the kind I'm

gonna get him. Everybody who's anybody knows that his wife was a tramp. I'm gonna let the little guy, the voters, know it, too."

"Before I hire you as McConnell's lawyer, I want to get one thing straight."

"What's that?"

"Your job is to get him free, not go after Richard Welles."

"I know that," Dundee said, "but if I can get Welles at the same time, that's what I'm gonna do. Agreed?"

"Whatever," Pike said. "Just get McConnell free."

"Sure," Dundee said. "Oh, by the way, did he do it?"

"No."

"Did he sleep with Mrs. Welles?"

"No."

"Did he know her?"

"No," Pike said, "we just go to town yesterday."

"All right," Dundee said, taking out a pad of paper, "tell me everything that happened from the time you first hit town—and don't leave anything out."

Pike thought a moment, then started talking . . .

When Pike stopped talking Dundee continued to write for a few minutes, then closed his pad and laid aside his pencil.

"This doesn't look good, you know."

"I know."

"Your friend was found in bed with her."

"He's not denying that," Pike said. "He just doesn't know how he got there."

"That's a little hard to believe," Dundee said, shaking his head.

"It's the truth!"

"Sure, sure," Dundee said, "and I believe you, but can you see a jury believing that?"

"A jury?"

"Your friend will be tried in front of twelve of St. Louis's finest citizens," Dundee said. "A jury. It will be them who decide whether he's guilty or not."

"What's the judge do?"

"He makes sure that nobody plays dirty."

"I thought that was your specialty."

"It is," Dundee said, grinning, "that's why judges and I don't see eye to eye." When Dundee said "eye to eye" he laid his right forefinger alongside his eye patch.

Dundee stood up and looked down at Pike.

"Is there anything you've left out?"

"No."

"Are you sure?"

"I'm positive."

"All right," Dundee said. "I have to go and talk to my client."

Pike started to stand up and Dundee put his hand on his shoulder again.

"You and I are gonna get along fine, Pike, as long as you never stand in my presence."

"Don't you want me to go with you?"

"No," Dundee said, patting Pike on the shoulder and then removing his hand, "I want to talk to McConnell alone." He looked at Pitch and said, "Thanks for the client referral, Joe."

"Anytime."

"You available to work for me?"

"As what?" Pike asked, looking at both men, puzzled.

"Didn't Joe tell you?" Dundee said. "He's a helluva detective."

"No, he didn't tell me."

"I ain't really—" Pitch started, but Dundee cut him off.

"Sure, he'd rather fight or tend bar, but he's a

78

detective, all right." He looked at Pitch and said, "You gonna work for me?"

"Sure."

"Go to the bar where McConnell waited for Pike, then, and see what you can find out."

"I did that already."

"No offense, Pike," Dundee said, "but it's just possible that you didn't ask all the right questions."

"Well, tell me what I can do to help."

"Do?" Dundee asked. "Stay out of the way, my friend. Let me and Joe Pitch handle it."

"I can't do that," Pike said. "Skins is my friend. I've got to do something."

"Why don't you go and do what you came here to do?" Dundee suggested. "Leave the rest to us. Joe, I'll meet you back here in three hours."

"Right."

"Gentlemen," Dundee said and started away.

"Mr. Dundee—" Pike said.

"Andy, Pike," Dundee said, "just call me Andy."

"Andy, we haven't talked about your pay—"

"We'll talk about it after," Dundee said. "Don't worry about it, Pike. It won't be more than you can afford."

As Dundee walked away Pike said, "How does he know what I can afford?"

"Don't worry about it," Pitch said. "Look, about this detective thing. I didn't recommend Dundee just so I could get a job out of it."

"I believe you," Pike said, "and it'd be fine even if you did. I like him."

"He'll give your partner a helluva defense," Pitch said. "Look, you wanna come to that bar with me? You're welcome to."

"But Andy said—"

"I'm working for Andy," Pitch said, "but I work my

way. Come on."

"If you're working for Andy," Pike said on the way out, "does that mean he's paying you?"

"Sure."

"Out of what I'm paying him?"

"I don't know where he gets the money he pays me, and I don't care," Pitch said. "Stop worrying about money, Pike. It ain't the most important thing in Andy Dundee's life."

"What about yours?"

"Me?" Pitch said. "Shit, I only use it to eat. Now shut up about it and tell me what you asked at this bar when you were there?"

PART THREE

THE INVESTIGATION

CHAPTER NINE

Pike walked back into the tavern with Joe Pitch, and the same bartender was behind the bar.

"Hello," the bartender said. "Find your friend?"

"Yeah, I found him," Pike said. "How about a couple of beers?"

"Sure."

They looked around the place and saw that it was less than half full. The bartender wasn't busy, so when he brought their beer Pike asked him to talk for a spell.

"Sure, why not?" the man said. "Did your friend have a good time yesterday, with that woman?"

"As a matter of fact," Pitch said, "he didn't. He was arrested for murder."

"What?" the man said. "That gal he left here with?"

"No, not her," Pitch said. "What's your name, friend?"

"I'm John Brenner."

"Well, John Brenner," Pitch said, "you read the papers, don't you?"

"Sure, I do," Brenner said. "Every morning—wait a minute. You mean to tell me . . ."

"That's right," Pitch said. "His friend, McConnell, was arrested for killing Mrs. Richard Welles."

83

"Well . . ." Brenner said, looking at Pike.

"He didn't do it," Pike said. "You saw him leave here with a woman."

"Yes."

"Was that woman Jennifer Welles?" Pitch asked.

"Now, what would Richard Welles's wife be doin' in here . . ."

"Then it wasn't?" Pitch asked.

"I . . . don't know—"

"You've seen her picture in the newspapers," Pitch said. "Was it her?"

Brenner stuck his right pinky into his ear and shook it around. The look on his face could have been one of pleasure, or pain.

"Were I pinned down," he said, finally, "I'd have to say no, it wasn't her—but that don't mean he couldn't have met up with her later, does it?"

"Are you a prosecutor?" Pitch asked.

"No, of course not—I just meant—"

"Mr. Pike here said something about two men, seated at a back table."

"That's right," Brenner said. "For a minute I thought the girl was gonna sit with them."

"Do you remember anything else about them?" Pitch asked. "Anything more than you remembered yesterday?"

"No . . ." Brenner said, rubbing his jaw, "I can't say as I do. Just that they were dressed like they were in business."

"Look," Pitch said, "I tend bar in the bar at the Carlyle Hotel. I know I remember regular customers who tip well, customers who won't pay. I remember customers who stand out. Are you telling me there was nothing about these two men that stood out?"

Brenner thought a moment, then said, "Nothing that

I can think of. They paid their bill. If they left a tip it wasn't one so large I would remember."

"Did they drink a lot?"

"I don't have a waitress here, but I don't remember going to their table more than once, maybe twice."

"Did they pay on the spot each time?"

"Yeah," Brenner said, "now that you mention it, they did pay for each round when I brought it."

"The same man pay both times?"

Brenner thought and said, "The older one, the one with white hair."

"And what did the other one look like?"

"Younger, slimmer, dark-haired—"

"Now we're getting somewhere," Pitch said, and Pike was impressed, because Joe Pitch was drawing all of this out of a man who said he couldn't remember anything.

"Tell me something about the white-haired man's hands," Pitch said.

"His hands?"

"Yes," Pitch said. "He paid both times, didn't he? You saw his hands?"

"Well, yes . . ."

"Tell me about them."

Brenner took a moment to look back inside his mind before speaking.

"A ring."

"What?" Pitch said.

"He wore a ring, on his right hand." Brenner looked surprised at himself, that he remembered this. "It was on his right hand."

"What kind of ring?"

"A gold one, with an initial on it."

"What was the initial?" Pitch asked.

Brenner thought, but shook his head.

"I'm sorry," he said, "that I can't remember."

"That's all right," Joe Pitch said. "You've remembered plenty. Now tell me this. Did you get the sense that they were strangers in town? Or citizens?"

"They were dressed like businessmen, but I had the feeling they weren't."

"Strangers? Visitors?"

"Both, I think," Brenner said.

"How do you know?"

"I don't know," Brenner said, "I think. That's the impression I got."

Pitch looked at Pike, as if to ask silently if he had any questions.

"Will you testify in court?"

"To what? I can't say what your friend did?"

"Just to what you said today."

Brenner shrugged and said, "Sure, why not?"

"Even knowing that if you testify for his friend, you'll be testifying against Richard Welles?" Pitch asked.

Brenner looked stunned for a moment.

"I never thought of it that way," Brenner said.

"Think about it," Pitch said. "We'll be back."

Pitch walked away from the bar and Brenner looked at Pike.

"No hard feelings if you decide not to," Pike said.

"Welles is a powerful man in this city," Brenner said. "Hell, in this state."

"I know," Pike said, "I know."

He dropped the money for the beers on the bar and followed Joe Pitch.

Outside he asked, "How did you get him to remember all of that?"

"He remembered it," Pitch said. "All I did was help him bring it to the surface."

"Do we have enough?"

"Enough to do what?"

"To find these men?"

"We have descriptions, and we have a ring," Pitch said. "I don't know if it's enough, but it's a hell of a lot more than we had before, isn't it?"

Leonard Roberts twisted the gold initial ring on his right hand with his left. The initial was "R".

"What do you think?" Cole asked.

"What harm can a mountain man do us here?" Roberts asked. "He's out of his element."

"We should have been more careful."

"We were careful," Roberts said. "The man we picked was obviously a stranger, obviously new in the city. From his appearance he was not only a stranger, but he was from the mountains. The chances were excellent that he had no family here with him."

"But he has a friend."

"We don't know that for sure," Roberts said, twisting the ring savagely, "but even if he does, what can the man do?"

"What are we supposed to do, then?" Cole asked. "Just forget it?"

Roberts took his hand away from his ring for a moment, then returned it.

"Follow him, then," Roberts said. "If you're worried about it, follow him, keep an eye on him. Let's see what he does."

"I don't know where he is."

"Go to his hotel, Bob, wait for him to either get there, or to come out, and then follow him. If he looks like he's going to be in one place for a length of time—like dinner—come and let me know what's going on."

"Len, we've got to leave St. Louis."

"I have to get our money," Roberts said, "and then we'll see."

"Len—"

"Go on, Bob," Roberts said.

Cole studied Roberts for a few moments, then turned and left the hotel room.

Leonard Roberts continued to twist his ring even after Cole left. Cole was nervous, and if he was right about McConnell having a friend, then maybe the police needed to know, without a doubt, who the killer was.

Maybe Roberts needed to give them Cole, and then get out of St. Louis himself.

Skins McConnell felt a whole lot better about his situation than he had in some time.

He'd gone to court that morning and had been virtually ignored by the judge, who had set his trial date at a week hence. His morale was at a new low when they took him back to his cell, but now that he had talked with Andy Dundee, he felt a lot better about his situation.

"You have to know," Dundee said, as he prepared to leave McConnell's cell, "Judge Meade and I don't get along, in court or out. He thinks I'm a drunken, worthless cuss who should be disbarred."

"And what do you think of him?" McConnell asked.

"I think he's a blight on the bench, and I'd love to get him kicked off. He's good friends with Richard Welles, which is going to make this doubly hard."

"Can't we get another judge?"

"Meade is a powerful man, Skins," Dundee said. "He'd block any attempts we made at getting a new judge assigned to this case."

88

"Then what do we do?"

"Do?" Dundee said. "We do the best we can, Skins. We raise Cain."

McConnell liked Andy Dundee. Even if he didn't beat this murder charge, it might end up being fun to try.

CHAPTER TEN

When Pike and Pitch returned to the hotel they went to the bar to wait for Dundee. The lawyer arrived twenty minutes later.

"I thought I was early," he said.

They ordered three beers and Dundee told them about his meeting with McConnell.

"I believe he didn't kill Mrs. Welles," Dundee said.

"That's good," Pitch said. "It will make it easier for you to defend him."

"Believe me," Dundee said, "it's not going to be easy to defend him, not with Judge Edward Meade on the bench."

"What's wrong with Meade?" Pike asked.

"First of all he hates my guts, and second of all he's in bed with Richard Welles—so to speak."

"I don't understand."

"He's one of Welles's biggest supporters."

"How did he end up the judge on Skins's case, then?" Pike asked. "That sounds like a conflict, to me."

"In this town, Judge Meade gets the cases he wants," Dundee said. "Nobody would have the nerve to question him on it."

"Except you," Pitch said.

Dundee smiled.

"That doesn't accomplish much," Dundee said. "Nobody listens to me. You know, it's quite a coincidence that this case will pit me against two of the men I respect the least in St. Louis."

"Just don't lose sight of your job," Pike said.

Dundee gave Pike a steely-eyed stare with his single eye and said, "I never forget my job, Mr. Pike."

"Sorry," Pike said, "but I'm worried about Skins."

"His spirits are good," Dundee assured Pike, "but you're wise to be worried. What did you find out at the bar, Joe?" he asked Pitch.

Pitch explained that he and Pike went over there, and then explained what he had drawn out of the bartender.

"Well, it's better than nothing," Dundee said. "Between you and me, Joe, we have enough contacts on the streets to spread these descriptions around."

"The streets?" Pike asked, thinking of the Sullivan brothers.

"Sure," Dundee said, "that's where most of my cases and most of my information come from. The people who live on the streets of a big city know more about it than anyone."

"If that's the case," Pike said, "I might have some contacts of my own."

"Good," Dundee said, "we're going to need all the help we can get."

"I'll get the descriptions out to the hotels," Joe Pitch said.

"All right," Dundee said. He finished his beer and stood up. "I have to get to work putting my case together. The trial's been set for a week from today, next Monday."

"Jesus," Pike said, "is that enough time to prepare?"

91

"It's going to have to be," Andy Dundee said, "isn't it?"

Pike spent some time in the bar talking with Joe Pitch, and then confessed to being hungry.

"So am I," Pitch said. "I know a place that has the best food in St. Louis. Interested?"

"In good food? Sure."

"It's not far," Pitch said. "When we get there you can tell me a little bit about this street source of yours. You've only been here a day, and already you have one?"

"They're just a couple of fellas I ran into," Pike said, truthfully.

Over dinner—which Pike could only describe as succulent—they exchanged life stories—at least, as much as each wanted to talk about their life. Pike generally considered that he had not even been born before he found his way to the Rockies as a very young man.

Pitch had worked in various jobs, usually jobs requiring a strong back. He discovered bartending quite by accident, and through that discovered that he was a good judge of people. Eventually, people began to ask him for help beyond his job as a bartender and he found himself acting in many cases as a detective. When he met Dundee, the lawyer began using him in the preparation of many of his defenses.

"I probably shouldn't ask this," Pike said, "but what is his record of success?"

Pitch made a face and said, "Considering how disliked he is by the police, by the judges and by other lawyers, it's pretty good."

"Somehow," Pike said, "I find that less than comforting."

"He'll give you his best, Pike," Joe Pitch said, "and that's as good as you'll get in St. Louis."

"Well, I guess I can't ask for more than that, can I?" Pike said.

Briefly, they discussed Pike's original reason for coming to St. Louis, and Pitch voiced the opinion that Pike should continue visiting the fur companies while Dundee and Pitch worked on clearing McConnell.

"I don't know if I can do that," Pike said.

"The way I see it, you have a responsibility to the people who sent you out here," Pitch said.

"I also have a responsibility to McConnell," Pike said. "I'm the one who talked him into coming here with me."

"That may be, but as I see it, you've done your best for him so far. You got him Dundee, and you got him me. What more could you do?"

Pitch meant to bring a smile to Pike's face with those remarks, but instead he got a serious comment from Pike.

"I went to see Richard Welles this morning."

"You did?" Pitch said, looking dubious. "I don't know if that was such a good idea. What happened?"

"He wasn't there," Pike said. "His sister, Lila, was, though."

"What's she like?"

"Well, I can't say whether she's like him or not, because I've never met, or even seen him. She's tall, very attractive, and very . . . forward."

"How do you mean, forward?"

Pike told Pitch about his visit, and Pitch's eyebrows went up.

"She's a flirt."

"I guess that's what you'd call her."

93

"There are other names for women like that, but we might as well stick with flirt until we know better," Pitch said. "How did you leave it?"

"I was supposed to go back this evening to see if her brother was home," Pike said. "In fact, it's not too late to do that."

"Let's hold off on that until tomorrow," Pitch said. "We'll talk to Andy about it. Maybe I'll go with you, or maybe he'll tell us not to go at all."

"Well, in that case, I guess I'd better turn in," Pike said.

"You turn in early in the mountains?"

"When we have nothing better to do."

"I know some bars we could stop at," Pitch said. "Are you interested in gambling?"

"Under normal circumstances, I'd say yes," Pike said.

"Come on," Pitch said. "Let me show you what St. Louis is like at night."

Pike thought about it for a moment, then nodded and said, "All right, why not? It's better than sitting in my hotel room worrying."

"Believe me, if your friend McConnell is the way you say he is, he wouldn't expect you to do that, would he?" Pitch said.

"No," Pike said, "he sure wouldn't."

"Then let's go," Pitch said. "There are beer mugs, cards and women waiting out there for us."

When Pike woke the next day there was a blond head down between his legs. The woman was avidly licking the length of his penis, which was ramrod straight and hard as a rock. He wondered how long she had been at it before he woke up.

Now that he was awake he was fully aware of the

sensations her silky tongue was causing. She was cupping his testicles in one hand while the other encircled the base of his penis. She obviously didn't know that he was awake, and didn't care. Suddenly, she lifted her head slightly, opened her mouth and engulfed him. He reached down to cup her head and she moaned as she began to suckle him.

Pike didn't remember who she was, where she came from or how they had gotten back to his room, but at that moment he didn't care. Hell, he didn't even know what she looked like, but that didn't matter, either. All that mattered was the explosion that was welling up in his loins, and when he finally let go and moaned again.

Whoever she was, she had the most amazing mouth!

"Oh, God," he said.

"Good morning," she said, looking up at him. Her face was thin, but not unattractive. Her mouth saved it. Her lips were thin, but her mouth was wide and, as she smiled at him, it transformed her face from plain to pretty.

She sat up and he saw that she was slender, with small, pink-tipped breasts partially obscured by a curtain of long hair, and she had a flat tummy. In fact, she could have used about ten or fifteen more pounds. She looked as if she hadn't been eating real well, lately.

"I'm Irma," she said.

He cleared his throat and said raggedly, "Good morning, Irma."

She smiled, touched her tousled hair and said, "I figured you wouldn't remember, not after all you drank last night."

"I drank a lot, huh?"

"More than I ever seen a man drink, honey, and then still be able to perform the way you did when we got back here."

"I performed, huh?"

"Oh, honey," she said, rolling her eyes. "You like to split me in two—not that I'm complaining, mind you. I like big men, myself, and you're about the biggest I ever been with—in more ways than one."

"I'll take that as a compliment."

Pike was still frowning, still taking stock of himself. They were in his room, and they must have spent all night in bed together, because his legs felt fatigued, as if he'd run all night. They must have really gone at each other, but Irma didn't look any the worse for wear.

"I hope you didn't mind me waking you up," she said, coyly.

"Oh, no," he said, "that was a fine way to wake, let me tell you."

"Well," she said, "now that you're awake I guess you want me to go, huh?"

He looked at her, and at her pink nipples, which were peeking at him through her golden hair. It was an erotic sight, and he felt himself beginning to react.

He didn't remember much of last night, which seemed a shame, because she seemed like a truly talented girl. She was obviously a prostitute, but he decided not to let her go until she had given him something he could really remember her by.

"No," he said, leaning forward, "I don't think so."

He used his forefinger to part the curtain of blond hair, exposing the pink nipple of her left breast. He leaned closer still and tongued the nipple. It reacted immediately, hardening, shrinking slightly as it became like a pebble. He closed his mouth over it and sucked it, reaching for the other breast with his hand and tweaking the nipple.

She slid her hand down his chest to his belly, rubbing him there, and then lower still, grasping his swelling penis.

He pushed her back, then, so that she was lying down

96

with her head at the bottom of the bed. He slid one hand down between her legs and when he found her wet and mounted her.

This was going to be a ride they both would remember.

Later, while she was dressing, Pike became aware of an ache in his left side, as if his ribs were sore.

"You didn't, uh, kick me in the ribs during the night, did you?"

"Honey," she said, "I did a lot of things to you during the night, but that wasn't one of them. Your ribs probably hurt because of the fight."

"Fight?" he said. "I had a fight?"

"You and your friend had a humdinger of a fight," she said. "You took on an entire bar all by yourselves. You were doing okay, too, while there were only twenty of them, but then five or six more came in and that was a little too much even for the two of you."

"Twenty?"

"More," she said, giving him an admiring look. "I never seen nothing like it before. Why, I saw seven or eight of them grab you and swallow you up. I could even see you until suddenly they all went flying, and there you was, your shirt all torn, shouting for more! You were beautiful!"

"I was, huh?"

"After they finally threw you out me and my friend went out to see if you and your friend were okay."

"And were we?"

"You were both sitting on the ground, laughing and slapping each other on the back. Your friend was bleeding from a cut over his eye, but he didn't seem to notice. Connie—that's my friend—she took him off to fix him up. You said you was okay, and you and I came here."

"Last night?"

"This morning, really, about two ay-yem."

"What time is it now?"

"About nine."

She had finished dressing and he saw that her dress was cheaply made, but cut to show off her charms to their best advantage.

"You need a new dress," he said.

She laughed and said, "Yeah, tell me about it."

He rolled over and found his pants on the the floor. He took out his money, gratified to see that it was all there, minus whatever they had drunk up last night. He took some and put the rest away, and then held it out to her.

"I tell you, mister," she said, eyeing the money, "I had such a good time last night I don't even know if I should take the money. Hell, maybe I should pay you. That was a fight worth payin' to see!"

"Take the money, Irma," he said. "Get yourself something pretty and buy yourself some food."

She moved forward, closed her hand over his with the money between them, and kissed him. Her tongue flicked out and licked his lips, and she straightened up with the money in her hand.

"Thanks, mister."

"Pike," he said.

"Thanks, Pike."

She walked to the door, then turned and said, "If you want me, you know where to find me," and left.

It was a few minutes before he realized that he still remembered nothing about last night, and *didn't* know where to find her at all.

CHAPTER ELEVEN

Pike staggered from his room, riddled with guilt over what had apparently been a helluva night's fun. Normally he enjoyed a good fight, and then a few hours with a willing woman, but he usually liked to remember it all the next day.

Now, even though he couldn't remember it, he felt guilty about doing it all while Skins McConnell was rotting in jail.

Even though the food in the hotel dining room was awful, he had breakfast there as a sort of punishment. While he was wading through the worst steak he'd ever seen, let alone eaten, Joe Pitch appeared at the door. He spotted Pike and walked over to his table. Pike was pleased to see that the whites of Pitch's eyes were more red than white.

"Have a seat," Pike said. "The food's terrible, but the coffee's even worse."

"As long as it's black and hot."

"It is that," Pike said, not bothering to tell Pitch that it was also thick, and filled with unground coffee grounds.

After Pitch took a long swallow of the vile, hot liquid he said, "Oh, what a night."

"You remember it?"

"Some of it," Pitch said. "Was there a fight?"

"I was gonna ask you that."

There was a scab over Pitch's right eye, so obviously what Irma had told him was true.

"I heard something about taking on a whole bar," Pike said. "Twenty or twenty-five men?"

"I heard fifty."

"Obviously, your whore exaggerated even more than mine did."

"Ah, yes," Pitch said, his face brightening, "Connie."

"And Irma."

"Mine was dark-haired."

"Mine was blond."

"Big tits and round hips?"

Pike shook his head.

"Small, and slender."

"Opposites, then."

"I guess so," Pike said, "but mine had a lot of energy."

"In that they were alike, then. I guess if they hadn't taken us home we never would have gotten there."

"I guess."

Pitch studied Pike for a few moments and said, "Feeling guilty over having a good time?"

"I'd probably feel more guilty if I could remember having a good time, but yeah, I am."

"Well, don't. We went through this last night. The last thing McConnell wants you to do is sit in your room and worry. I'm tellin' you. Go on about your business, and we'll take care of him."

"Where's Dundee's office?"

Pitch stared at Pike.

"You didn't hear a word I said, did you?"

"I heard you," Pike said. "Where is Dundee's office?"

"Why?"

"I want to talk to him."

"About going to see Welles?"

"Yeah."

"All right," Pitch said. "Finish your . . . whatever it is you're eating . . . and I'll take you over there."

"I'm finished," Pike said, pushing away from the table, "but you don't have to take me over there. Just tell me where it is."

"Believe me," Pitch said, grinning, "even a big fella like you don't want to go to that neighborhood alone."

Robert Cole saw Pike leave the hotel in the company of another man. The second man was brawny enough to be a mountain man, but he sure didn't dress like one. It looked to Cole like Pike had made a friend in St. Louis.

In a brief moment of panic Cole wondered if the other man was a policeman. Should he follow anyway? What would he tell Leonard Roberts if he didn't? That he was afraid to? Even if the other man was a policeman, there was no law against walking on the street.

He decided to go ahead and follow them.

Leonard Roberts checked his watch. In one hour he was due to go and collect the money for the job on Jennifer Welles.

In an hour and a half he was going to have to decide what he was going to do about Cole, who was entirely too nervous these days.

When they reached the area where Dundee's office was located Pike saw what Pitch meant about the

101

neighborhood. It was the most rundown part of St. Louis he had seen yet, except for the shanty town they had passed on the way from the train station. The buildings were all wooden, and in a state of disrepair. On the street the people were much the same. As Pike and Pitch walked by they begged for food, or coins, or anything the two men would deign to give them.

"Don't give them anything," Pitch said.

"Why not?" Pike said. "They look like they need a lot of help."

"They do," Pitch said, "but if you give one, you got to give them all. Can you support every homeless or drunken person in St. Louis?"

"No."

"There's his building."

Pitch pointed to a building with broken windows on both of its floors. The windows on the main floor were boarded up.

"His office is on the main floor."

When they reached the front door Pike saw that there was no doorknob, just a makeshift wooden handle.

"Why does he have an office here?" Pike asked.

"He was born here," Pitch said. "Come on."

Pitch opened the door and they entered. The inside wasn't much better than the outside. There was a worn sofa and a battered desk. Sitting at the battered desk was Andy Dundee, his sleeves rolled up, the desk filled with papers. Pike couldn't even tell which piece of paper the man was reading.

"Andy," Pitch said.

Dundee looked up and the look on his face made it clear that he hadn't heard him enter.

"Hello, fellas."

From the look of Dundee's one eye, he had been there all night.

102

"Didn't you go home last night?" Pitch asked.

"Naw," Dundee said, rubbing his face, "I caught some sleep on the sofa. What can I do for you?"

"Pike has something he wants to ask you about."

"Oh?" Dundee said. "What is it?"

Pike told Dundee about going to see Richard Welles and talking to his sister.

"I was supposed to go back yesterday evening, but I was kidnapped." Pike gave Pitch a pointed look.

"I did not kidnap you."

"I know," Pike said.

They both looked at Dundee, who seemed to have forgotten they were there. He was staring off into space.

"Andy?" Pitch said.

Without looking at either one of them Dundee said, "Go ahead."

"What?" Pitch asked.

Now Dundee looked up at Pike.

"You want to know if you should go and see Richard Welles, right?"

"Right."

"I say go ahead."

"You don't see a problem in that?" Pitch asked, obviously surprised at Dundee's reaction.

"Sure," Dundee said, "but what the hell." He looked at Pike and said, "Go and see him, Pike, and let's see what happens."

"What could happen?" Pike asked.

"Oh, I guess the worse he could do is send someone to kill you."

"If he does that," Pike said, "won't that mean he's guilty of something?"

"It might," Dundee said, "it just might."

*   *   *

103

Cole was confused.

What were the mountain man and the other man doing in a building in this neighborhood? And where was the mountain man going now that he had left alone?

There was only one way to find that out, so Cole continued to follow him.

At least he didn't have to worry about the other man, whether he was a policeman or not.

Pike left Pitch at Dundee's office. The two men wanted to discuss strategy. Dundee wanted Pike to get back to him after he saw Richard Welles. Pike hoped he was getting to the Welles house early enough to catch the man in.

When he reached the house he knocked on the door, and turned around to look at the street while he waited for an answer. He saw a man across the street slip into a doorway. The man looked familiar, as if he had seen him before, recently, but he couldn't place him at the moment. When the door opened he turned, forgetting about the man for the moment.

"Well, Mr. Pike," Lila Welles said. "Your timing is perfect."

"Meaning?"

"Well, it could mean that I was just in the mood for a big man," Lila said with a flirtatious smile, "but the fact of the matter is my brother is home."

"Did you tell him I was here yesterday?"

"I did not," she said. "I wanted it to be a surprise. Please, come in."

Once again she did not move aside to allow him entry. This time he decided that if she wanted to rub bodies he was all for it. You couldn't have fit a breeze

104

between them as he squeezed through the doorway.

"Oooh," she said, and closed the door. He noticed that her breathing had quickened. "This way, please."

She walked ahead of him and he enjoyed the way she did it as he followed her.

"Richard," she said, entering the library, "there's a man here to see you."

"Damn it, Lila," Welles said, annoyed, "I don't have any appointments at home today."

"I know, dear," Lila said, undaunted, "but I thought you might like to speak to this man. It's about Jennifer."

"Eh? What about Jennifer?"

"Mr. Pike," Lila said. This time she did step aside to allow him to enter the library.

"What's your connection to my wife?" Welles demanded immediately.

Pike took a moment to commit Richard Welles to memory. The man was tall, over six feet, though not as tall as Pike, and he was spare, almost painfully thin. He had dark hair, pale skin with no hint of beard. His face still showed the redness of a recent shave. Though he was standing straight, he looked as if he were slightly bent forward. He appeared to be in his forties, but when you're that slender you can carry it well, and he did. Pike thought that if women voted, he was assured of winning.

"I asked you what you had to do with my wife," Welles said, growing more agitated.

"Nothing."

"Nothing?" Welles repeated. He looked at his sister and said, "Lila, is this a joke?"

"This is no joke, Mr. Welles," Pike said. "I don't have any connection with your wife. I didn't even know her—but then, neither did Skins McConnell."

105

"McConnell?" Welles said, his face flushing. "The man who killed my wife? What have you to do with him?"

"We're friends," Pike said. "We both came to St. Louis day before yesterday. He was arrested the same day for killing your wife, but he wasn't here long enough to know her. I can testify to that."

None of the three people in the room spoke then. They all had reason to believe that it didn't take Jennifer Welles very long to get to know a man.

"The police have a very good case, Mr. . . ."

"Pike," Lila said.

"Yes, Mr. Pike," Welles said. "Your friend was found in bed with my wife's body."

"He has no idea how he got there," Pike said.

"Oh, come now—"

"We believe he was knocked unconscious and placed in the bed next to your wife."

"That is a lame story, Mr. Pike, and one I can assure you will hold no water with the judge."

"I thought the jury decided the case."

"That's true," Welles said, "but the judge oversees the jury. He will not allow them to perpetrate a travesty such as letting your friend go."

"But he didn't do it."

"Then get a lawyer and prove it in court," Welles said. He picked up a dark jacket and slid it on over his boiled white shirt and his black vest. He looked like some gamblers who came to the mountains at times to pick the trappers clean at rendezvous.

"We have a lawyer," Pike said.

"Who, may I ask, took this hopeless case?" Welles asked.

"Andrew Dundee."

Welles almost choked as he blurted, "Dundee? That incompetent . . . that poor excuse for a man . . .

106

and a lawyer?"

Pike smiled at Welles and said, "We like him."

"I can tell you, Mr. Pike, you are doing your friend no good service by hiring Andrew Dundee."

"What do you care?" Pike asked. "You want him convicted of the murder, don't you?"

Welles took a few steps which brought him fairly close to Pike. He showed Pike an exceptionally long forefinger.

"I want him convicted because he is guilty," Welles said.

"And you've got just the judge that will do that for you, don't you, Mr. Welles?"

"I don't know what—"

"Let me tell you something, Welles," Pike said, showing a pretty long forefinger of his own, "I not only plan to clear my friend, but I'm gonna find out who really did kill your wife. I only hope you're around to thank me when I do find him."

"Is that a threat?" Welles turned to Lila and said, "You heard him, Lila, he threatened me?"

"What was that, dear?" Lila asked, blinking rapidly. "I'm sorry, I wasn't listening."

Welles glared at his sister, then brushed past Pike and said, "Excuse me, but I am late for an appointment."

Pike turned and watched the man stalk down the hall and out of sight. Moments later the front door slammed.

Pike turned to Lila Welles, who looked amused by the whole thing, and said, "Why do I get the feeling that you feel less than sorry for your brother?"

"My brother gets a little pompous at times," she said. "He needs to be taken down a peg or two. I enjoyed watching you do it."

"I see."

"Have you any pressing engagements today, Mr. Pike?"

"Engagements? Oh, no, I don't have any appointments, if that's what you mean."

"That's what I mean," she said. She licked her generous mouth and moved closer to him. "What would you say to coming upstairs with me?"

"Uh, for what?"

"Well," she said, "I don't know how they say it in the mountains, but I'd like you to make love to me until I'm black and blue."

"Uh . . ." Pike said, taken aback.

"Don't men and women make love in the mountains?" she asked.

"Of course—"

"Still shocked at my frankness, Mr. Pike?"

"Frankly, Miss Welles," Pike said, "also by your language."

"What about my offer?"

He smiled, realizing that she was serious, and said, "Best one I've had all day."

Cole was biting his thumbnail when he saw Welles leave the house. The big mountain man was still inside. Why was that? Was there someone else in there? Had Welles asked him to stay?

Cole waited a few minutes to see if Pike would leave, and when the big man didn't, he decided to cross the street and take a look.

Leonard Roberts saw Welles leave his house, and saw Cole cross the street. Obviously, this was not the time to get paid.

He turned and left, leaving the following to Cole.

CHAPTER TWELVE

It was a helluva a way to spend a morning.

When noon came around Lila Welles was seated astride Pike, his rigid cock buried deeply inside of her. She had the uncanny ability to flex the muscles of her insides so that he felt as if a hand were tugging at him, literally yanking an ejaculation from him. As he spurted inside of her, her head fell back on her neck and he reached up to cup her large breasts, popping the nipples with his thumbs.

When the waves of pleasure and sensation abated she fell flat atop him, crushing her breasts against his hard chest.

"Jesus," she said, panting.

"Are you black and blue yet?" he asked.

She laughed into his neck and said, "Almost lover, almost there."

She allowed his semi-erect penis to slide free of her, then slid down and licked him clean, like a cat. When he was clean, however, she continued to lick him, until his cock wasn't just semi-erect, but fully hard again.

She turned around, presenting her ample butt to him and, looking over her shoulder at him said, "After *this* I'll be black and blue."

He shook his head, amazed at her stamina, and pleased that his own seemed to be matching it—especially after the night he'd spent with Irma.

He knelt behind her, palmed her firm buttocks, and drove himself home . . .

As they dressed he asked, "Will you be staying here with your brother?"

"For a while," she said.

"Why?"

"I beg your pardon?"

"You obviously aren't mourning your sister-in-law, and you don't seem to be giving your brother much sympathy."

"Just because we've made love for three hours doesn't mean you know me, Pike," she said. He found it odd that she would become insulted. "He's still my brother. No matter how I feel about him, he's my only family."

Pike took a shot in the dark.

"He holds the family purse strings, huh?"

She stared at him for a full two minutes, and then a sheepish smile spread over her lovely face.

"Daddy left him every penny," she said, shaking her head. "Good guess, Pike."

"Why didn't Daddy leave you any of the money?"

"Daddy loved me," she said, "I was his little girl, but he didn't like my life style. I do have some money, but Richard controls that, too. My allowance gets smaller and smaller."

"You think he'll be more generous now that his wife is dead?"

"Hardly," she said, "but there's always a chance. Come downstairs and I'll give you a drink."

They went downstairs and she poured herself a

brandy and him a whiskey.

"What did you think of my brother?" she asked.

"I didn't like him."

"That makes you even," she said. "I don't think he liked you, either."

"Is that why you took me upstairs? Because he didn't like me?"

"Don't be so modest," she said. "You know why I took you upstairs. I liked you—I wanted you—the moment I saw you."

"Because I'm so good-looking?"

"Now don't be immodest," she said. "You know you're not good-looking—but you are big, the kind of big that is a challenge to some women."

"Women like you?"

"Exactly," she said. "I wanted to climb you the moment I saw you. Couldn't you tell?"

He didn't answer.

"Come on," she said, "a man can tell."

"Where was your brother the night his wife was killed?" Pike asked.

She stared at him for a moment and then said, "Oh, very good, Pike. You may not be a detective, but you classify as a world class sneak. Trying to get me to implicate my brother?"

"Why? Can you implicate him?"

"Even if I could, I wouldn't."

"Why not? Maybe he killed her."

"This may shock your mountain man sensibilities, Pike, but I don't care if he killed her."

"But if he did, and he went to jail, wouldn't you get the money?"

She smiled and shook her head.

"Sneaky, sneaky, ever sneaky. No, the money would still be his, and I'd have to deal with his lawyers to get even a penny."

"So if he did it, you wouldn't say?"

"No," she said. "In fact, if he did it I'd give him a medal."

"Why?"

"Jennifer had the morals of an alley cat," Lila said. "She'd spread her legs for any pair of pants who came along—I know," she said, quickly, before Pike could say anything, "after what we did upstairs you don't think I'm much better, and you might be right, but at least I'm discreet. Her tomcatting might have cost Richard the election."

"And if he wins the election, he might be in a generous mood?"

"Who ever said mountain men were dumb?"

"Not me," he said. He finished his whiskey and put the glass down.

"Are you leaving?"

"I have to," he said. "If you're not going to help me, I'll have to look for help somewhere else."

"Like where?"

He shrugged and said, "Maybe on the streets."

"Well, there's one thing you won't have to look on the street for," she said.

She put her brandy glass down, moved close to him and drew his head down so she could kiss him, a long, wet, tongue-lashing, toe-curling kiss.

"You know where to find me," she said.

As he left he realized that she was the second woman to tell him that today—but at least he did know where to find this one.

Cole saw them kiss, and as the big man turned to leave he hurried away from the house, back across the street. He had not seen what went on in the upstairs room, but he could guess. He wondered who the

112

woman was. Was Welles keeping a woman in his house so soon after his wife's death?

He watched from the doorway as Pike left the house and walked down the street. He stepped out and followed at what he considered a discreet distance.

After Jack Pike left the house Lila Welles poured herself another, stiffer brandy. After she drank that down she realized she needed something stronger, and had some of the whiskey that Pike had drunk.

That done, she went upstairs to make the bed in Richard's room. She wondered what he would think if he knew what had gone on in *his* bed that morning.

Maybe she'd leave it just messy enough to give him a hint.

When Richard Welles reached his offices he called his aide into his private office.

George Belson entered behind his boss.

"The mayor wants to—"

"Forget that for now."

"Forget the mayor?"

"George!" Welles's voice was like cold steel.

George Belson was young, in his late twenties, and was considered a comer in St. Louis politics. He intended to ride Richard Welles's coattails to his own success. Part of that, right now, was snapping to whenever Welles exhibited that tone of voice.

"Yes, sir."

"There's a man named Pike, he's connected with that man McConnell—"

"The one who killed your wife?"

"Yes, who else do we know named McConnell!"

Belson fell silent and listened.

"I want you to find out where Pike is staying."

"Uh, okay," Belson said, "but, uh, how exactly do I do that?"

"George—" Welles said, shaking his head. His intention had been to scold the younger man, but he changed his mind. Wearily, he said, "Talk to Lieutenant Healy, he can probably help you."

"Right, that's right," Belson said, snapping his fingers and wondering why he hadn't thought of that. "I'll talk to Healy."

"Don't talk to anyone else," Welles said. "Find out where Pike is staying and get back to me right away, understand?"

"Yes, sir," George Belson said. "I understand perfectly."

"Then get to it."

"Yes, sir," Belson said. "Now about the mayor. He wanted you to—"

"Do what I told you to do," Welles said, tightly, "and to hell with the mayor!"

As Pike left the Welles house he spotted the man across the street again. It struck him then that the man seemed familiar to him because he had seen him on the street several times over the past two days, invariably somewhere behind him.

Suddenly, after two days, he knew he was being followed.

Who ever said mountain men were dumb?

CHAPTER THIRTEEN

Now that Pike knew he was being followed he had to decide what to do about it. Ideally, he would have liked to ask the man who sent him, and why he was following him. To do that, however, he had to get his hands on him. If he turned and ran toward the man, he wasn't sure he could catch him. He was going to have to make the man come to him.

He decided to lead the man back to his hotel. There he could figure out a way of maybe getting behind him.

He entered the lobby and noticed that the man did not enter behind him. He went directly to the desk.

"Is there a back way out of here?" he asked the desk clerk.

"Uh, yes, sir," the man said, frowning. "There are two. There is one through the kitchen, and another through this hall behind the desk." He was indicating a curtained doorway directly behind the desk.

"Good," Pike said, starting around the desk.

"Sir," the clerk said, "you come back here—"

"I'll only be a minute," Pike assured him. He brushed the clerk aside and went through the curtained doorway. He found himself in a hallway and took it to the end, passing several offices along the way. Finally, he came to a door. He opened it and stepped through, found himself in another hallway. This one led to a back door that opened onto an alley.

Now that he was outside he hoped that the man who was following him was still waiting for him in front of the hotel.

Leonard Roberts saw Pike come down the street toward his hotel, and behind him Bob Cole. He watched as Pike entered the hotel and Cole took up a position across the way.

By this time the big mountain man must have known that he was being followed.

It was time for Roberts to act.

Pike looked both ways and saw that the alley was open on both sides. It didn't much matter which direction he took, so he chose right. When he came out on a small side street next to the hotel he made another right and walked to the corner. He peered around the corner and saw his man, leaning in a doorway across from the hotel's front entrance. The man did not see him, because he was concentrating on the entrance.

Pike first crossed the side street, then sticking close to the store fronts he stepped out onto the main street and walked quickly away from the hotel. When he felt he was a safe enough distance away, he crossed over. Now that he was on the same side of the street as his man he started back toward the hotel, again staying close to the store fronts for cover.

Before long he was only five doorways away from the man who was watching the hotel.

Then four, and the man still hadn't moved.

Three . . . and the man was just standing there, his

head turned toward the hotel.

Two doorways . . .

And then one . . .

Pike reached out and grabbed the man by the front of his jacket.

"All right, friend," he said, yanking the man out of the doorway, "start talking—"

He stopped short, however, when the man fell forward. Pike held onto his jacket, keeping the man from hitting the ground.

"What the—" he said, behind over the man. He saw the crimson slash across his throat, and noticed now that the front of his shirt was soaked with blood.

Gently, he lowered the dead man to the ground.

"Hey!" someone shouted. "He's killed him! Get the police!"

Pike looked up and saw that several people across the street had stopped walking and were staring at him. He couldn't tell which of them had yelled.

"Police!" a woman began to shout. "Police!"

Pike looked down at the body, and then at the gathering crowds of people across the street, and now on his side of the street as well.

He knew what it looked like, and he knew there was no use in trying to talk to them. Running was out, as well. He was too distinctive a figure not to be identified easily. He knew what he had to do.

He had to wait for the police to arrive, and try and talk his way out of this.

"This doesn't look good for you, Pike," Inspector Emerson said. "I hope you know that."

"I don't know," Pike said. "I'm pretty pleased with the way it's gone so far, Inspector."

"What do you mean?"

"I could be in here talking to Lieutenant Healy instead of you."

"Healy doesn't like you."

"I guessed that."

"But then there aren't a whole lot of people he does like."

"Unless they're rich and powerful."

Emerson smiled in spite of himself.

"You're right about that. All right, tell it to me again."

It actually was not as bad as it could have been, Pike thought, even as he recited the story to Emerson all over again. No one had actually seen Pike kill the man—who was, as of now, unidentified—and there had not been a knife on him when the police arrived. Also, the police could not find a knife in the area. If Pike had killed the man, where was the knife?

Emerson was at least civil, and reasonable. If Healy had been on duty instead, Pike was sure he'd be in a cell right next to McConnell.

"So you figure the man's been following you for two days?"

"Near as I can figure."

"And you never saw him before this?"

"I must have glimpsed him from time to time, but he just didn't register."

"And today he did."

"Yes."

"And you never saw him before you came to St. Louis?" Emerson asked.

"Well, I never saw him in the mountains," Pike said. "I can't say for sure whether he was on the train with us, or not."

They were in Emerson's office, and the inspector was seated behind his desk. Pike was seated in a straight-backed wooden chair, and there were no chains on him.

118

Not yet, anyway.

"Look, Inspector," Pike said, "I've told you this over and over. I led him back to my hotel so I could circle around him and get some answers. By the time I got to him, he was dead, propped up in the doorway."

"Why would someone kill him and prop him up like that?" Emerson asked.

"So they could make it look like I killed him," Pike answered. "I told you, someone shouted, 'he killed him,' and then the crowds started to gather."

"All right, Pike," Emerson said, "suppose you tell me what you think happened?"

"I think someone was waiting for us at the hotel," Pike said. "I think that someone killed this man, and then stayed around to shout 'he killed him,' and then disappeared in the crowd."

"Why?"

"I wish I knew," Pike said.

"Who have you gotten mad at you since you've been in town?"

"Well, Healy for one."

"Who else?"

"No one . . . unless you count Richard Welles."

Emerson's eyes narrowed and he sat forward in his chair.

"What about Richard Welles?"

"I was at his house this morning, asking him some questions."

"About what?"

"His wife."

"I thought I told you—"

"I know what you told me, Inspector, but I had to do something for McConnell."

"What happened with Welles?"

"Nothing much. We talked a while, and then he left for an appointment."

"And he was angry?"

"Well, he wasn't pleased."

"Damn," Emerson said.

At that point the door slammed open and Lieutenant Jerry Healy walked in.

"Why isn't this man in a cell?" he demanded.

Inspector Earl Emerson stood up and stared icily at Healy.

"First of all, Lieutenant, you knock before you enter my office. Is that clear?"

Healy took his eyes from Pike, glared at Emerson for a long moment, and then said, "Yes, sir."

"Secondly, what the hell are you doing here?"

"I was informed that this man was harassing Richard Welles this morning . . . in his own home!"

"Oh? And who informed you of this?"

"Mrs. Welles's assistant, George Belson."

"Has Welles made a complaint against Mr. Pike?"

Healy tossed Emerson an icy stare and said, "Mr. Welles has not."

"Then what are you doing here?"

"I want this man locked up—"

"Well, we can't very well lock him up just because you want it that way, can we?"

"What about the murder?"

"What murder?"

"Pike killed a man today—"

"Where did you hear that?"

"I heard it when I came in."

"Then you must have heard that Mr. Pike is here being questioned about a murder that happened across the street from his hotel. He has not been charged with anything, at this point."

"Are you going to let him walk out of here?"

"I don't have any evidence that he did anything but discover a dead body, and the last time I looked,

Lieutenant, that wasn't against the law."

Healy glared at Pike, then stared at Emerson.

"You won't get away with this," Healy finally said. Pike wasn't sure which of them he was talking to. "The chief will hear about this."

"That's fine," Emerson said, "you go to the chief. You do whatever you have to do, as long as you get out of my office . . . now!"

Healy's stares were getting monotonous by this time, but he graced each of them with another before he went storming out.

Emerson looked at Pike, who looked up at the man from his seat and said, "I guess he doesn't like you, either, huh?"

He stood up and started walking toward the door.

"Where the hell do you think you're going?" Emerson shouted.

Pike turned, looking confused.

"I was leaving."

"I didn't tell you to leave."

"But I thought you said—"

"I said you were being questioned about a murder," Emerson said. "I never said you could leave. Sit your ass back down, Pike. I'm not through with you, yet!"

CHAPTER FOURTEEN

Pike could tell from the cold look in Emerson's eyes that he wasn't kidding, so he sat his ass back down and waited.

"Healy and I have never gotten along," Emerson said. "That doesn't mean that you're gonna walk out of here just because he wants me to lock you up."

"I didn't think that."

"The hell you didn't."

"Well, maybe I did."

Emerson sat down again and seemed to be making an effort to calm himself down. Pike wasn't sure if the man was fuming because of him, or because of Lieutenant Healy.

"Why don't you and Healy get along?" he asked. He got tired of waiting.

"I'm a policeman," Emerson said.

"So's he."

"He," Emerson said slowly, "is a damned politician."

"Oh."

"You haven't met very many politicians, have you, Pike?"

"I have to admit," Pike said, "we don't have that many in the mountains."

"Well, be glad about that," Emerson said. "Sometimes I wish they were an endangered species, like the beaver."

Pike sat up straight and said, "Who told you the beaver was endangered?"

"If they weren't, would you be here? By the way, have you done anything about that?"

"Not since McConnell was arrested," Pike said, immediately feeling guilty.

"I'll tell you what," Emerson said, "I'll make you a deal."

"What kind of a deal?"

"I'll let you walk out of here if you promise to go and see those fur companies you came to see."

Pike frowned.

"Why would you do that?"

"Because," Emerson said, "if you're bothering the fur companies, you won't be bothering me."

Pike could have argued the point, but decided instead to simply agree with it.

"Okay."

Emerson frowned.

"You agreed to that pretty easily, but I'll take you at your word."

"I promise," Pike said, "I'll go and see the fur companies."

"All right," Emerson said. "I'm not going to hold you, Pike—I could, though. You understand that, don't you?"

"Sure."

"Go on," Emerson said, "get out of here."

"Can I see McConnell?"

"No," Emerson said, "he's got a lawyer now, and he's the only one who gets in to see him."

"Why's that?"

"Because," Emerson said, averting his eyes, "that's

the way the chief wants it."

"The chief?" Pike asked, standing up, "or the judge? Or Richard Welles?"

Emerson shrugged and said, "It's all the same to me. Go on, get out of here, before I change my mind."

"I'm going, Inspector," Pike said. "Thanks."

"Do me a favor," Emerson called out at the last minute.

"What?" Pike asked, all but his head out the door.

"If you see Healy on the way out?"

"Stay out of his way?"

"No," Emerson said, "grin at him."

Pike didn't see Healy on the way out, which was fine with him. He went to his hotel to take a bath and change into fresh clothes. When he discovered that he didn't have any fresh clothes, he went out and bought a pair of gray serge pants and a boiled white shirt. The clothing felt odd and alien against his flesh, but he supposed he could get used to it.

He did as Inspector Emerson asked him to do; he went to see the heads of the other two fur companies, the North American and Rocky Mountain Fur Companies.

Neither company was as large as Hudson Bay, but in each case the man Pike spoke to was more sympathetic than the Hudson Bay man had been. Maybe the smaller the company, the more sympathy the hunters and trappers would get.

Sympathy was, however, all he got. Neither company promised to increase their offers to the mountain men, although both said they would take it under advisement. Both were also willing to talk to Pike again in a couple of days, after they had considered his plight. It was odd, but they had both said exactly that, his "plight."

After leaving the third company, Pike started to

think about Skins McConnell's "plight." He had kept his word to Emerson, and had spoken to the other two fur companies.

That was all he had promised to do.

When he went back to the hotel he found someone waiting for him in the lobby.

"What are you doing here?" he asked.

Lila Welles smiled and shrugged.

"I'm not sure."

"Do you want to come upstairs?"

"That wouldn't be discreet, would it?"

"No."

"You look different."

"It's the clothes," he said. "They're new. They're not exactly my size, but at least they're new."

"I know a tailor who could fit you perfectly," she said, touching the sleeve of the shirt.

"Uh, no thanks," Pike said. "I'm hoping I won't be here long enough to need new clothes that fit perfectly."

He looked her up and down and saw that her clothes fit her pretty perfectly. She was wearing a dress that outlined her womanly figure, and a shawl over it. Her hair was black and lustrous, hanging over both shoulders down over her breasts.

"Well," she said, "maybe I'll get you a jacket. You should have a jacket to go with that white shirt."

"Would you like to have some coffee?" he asked. "It's terrible here, but . . ."

"That's all right," she said. "I don't like coffee, anyway."

"How about some tea?" he asked. "How could they ruin tea?"

"I don't know," she said. "Suppose we find out?"

Pike had coffee, Lila had tea, and after an hour he still didn't know why she had come there.

"Well," she said, "I have to get back to the house before Richard misses me."

"Why?"

Standing she said, "Well, if he knew I was here with you . . ." and shrugged.

He stood and said, "Thank you for the company."

"Thank you for the tea," she said. "It was an experience."

"Why?"

"We actually found a place that can ruin tea."

He watched her leave and then sat back down.

Why would a woman sleep with him in her brother's house with no worries, and then worry that her brother might find out they had tea together?

And what had she wanted? In an hour all they did was exchange small talk. Was there something she had wanted to ask him, only to back out when the moment came?

Or was she keeping him busy down here for another reason?

He stood up, left the dining room and hurried up to his room. When he got there he saw that the door was ajar. He removed the Kentucky pistol from his belt and nudged the door open with the barrel. There was no one inside, but someone had been there recently. He wasn't a neat man, but he had not left this much of a mess.

He put the pistol down on the dresser and closed the door, locking it. Both his things and McConnell's were spread over the bed and on the floor. Someone had been looking for something, but what? And who? And had Lila been keeping him busy downstairs while they looked for it?

He'd have to ask her the next time he saw her.

*   *   *

Leonard Roberts didn't have a partner any more.

He also hadn't been paid for killing Jennifer Welles yet, which bothered him. He had gone to his employer's house, but no one had answered the door, so here he was back at his hotel, staring out the window, wondering if someone might be planning not to pay him.

If someone was, it would be the biggest mistake of their life.

Richard Welles looked up from his desk when George Belson entered his office.

"What?"

"All we know about him is that his name is Jack Pike and he came here from the mountains to talk to some of the fur companies."

"About what?"

"Apparently, they have lowered the prices that they've been paying the mountain men for skins and such. Pike is here to try and get them to reconsider."

"And McConnell?"

"Came along for the ride, I guess."

"You guess?" Welles said.

"I can't say for certain. Whatever the reason, he's here and he killed your wife. He'll pay for it."

"Get out."

"Sir—"

"Get out!" Welles said.

"Yes, sir."

Welles sat back in his chair and gnawed on a thumbnail. It was a habit he was trying to break. He only did it now when he was alone.

Pike worried him. If the big mountain man kept poking into his affairs, who knew what he'd turn up?

"Belson!"

The aide appeared at the door instantly.

"Yes, sir?"

"Get me Healy."

"Here, sir?"

"Of course here, man, where do you think?" Welles said, showing his exasperation. "Now get to it. I want him here within the hour."

"Yes, sir," Belson said. "Right away."

Pike had to be removed, and Healy was the man to see to it.

Lila returned to the Welles house. She dropped her shawl onto the sofa and poured herself a glass of brandy. She had felt like a fool the entire time she was at Pike's hotel. What must he have thought of her, rambling on like that incessantly, and not once saying anything of interest to anyone, let alone a man from the mountains.

She finished the brandy and poured another. When Richard came home they were going to have a long talk.

After Pike finished cleaning up the room he changed back into his buckskins and went out onto the street. He had not seen the Sullivan boys since that night he'd bought them dinner, and he didn't really know where to start looking for them.

They lived on the streets, though, so if he walked enough of them, maybe he'd find them.

"Remove him?" Lieutenant Jerry Healy repeated.

"You know what I mean, Healy," Richard Welles said. "Let's don't get dense now."

"But, sir . . ." Healy stammered, "I don't do that sort of thing—I mean—" He was standing before the Great Man himself, in his office, having been called there on an urgent matter.

"I'm not saying do it yourself, man!" Welles said. If he closed his eyes he'd swear he was talking to George Belson, again. "Have it done."

In his mind Jerry Healy always referred to Richard Welles as the "Great Man," because that was what he thought, that Welles was a great man who could do great things for the state of Missouri—and for Jerry Healy's career.

"How?"

"I don't care how," Welles said. "Look, do you want a career in politics or not?"

"Of course I do—"

"Then you'd better learn to do political favors," Welles said. He continued, lowering his voice and making his tone a more friendly one. "Consider this a political as well as a personal favor to me, Jerry."

He stood up, walked around his desk and put his arm around Healy's shoulders.

"When I'm governor, Jerry, I'm going to need men like you," he continued, his tone even more cajoling. "Decisive men who aren't afraid to take whatever action is necessary. Do you understand me?"

"Of course, sir." Welles could feel Healy's spine stiffen. "I understand perfectly."

Of all the things Healy wanted to ask was, why? What was it about Pike that so threatened the next governor of Missouri?

But he didn't ask.

"I'll take care of it, sir," he said. "Don't worry about it."

"I won't, Jerry." Welles removed his arm and clapped Healy on the shoulder in a gesture of comradeship. "I won't worry, Jerry, because I know you can handle this matter for me."

"I'll get on it immediately, sir," Healy said.

"Good, Jerry, good," Welles said, moving back around his desk as Healy moved for the door. "And Jerry?"

"Yes, sir?"

"Don't come here after it's, er, done," Welles said. "I'll have someone contact you for all the details. All right?"

"Whatever you say, sir."

"All right," Welles said, and Healy left.

For a moment Welles wondered if he shouldn't have brought in a professional for the job, but that would have taken time. Hopefully, Healy would be able to get some men who would be able to do the job competently.

Surely a lieutenant of police would know such men.

PART FOUR

HIRED GUNS

CHAPTER FIFTEEN

Pike walked the streets of St. Louis, keeping his eye out for the Sullivan boys. At one point, when it seemed he'd never find them, he started pressing money into the hands of the homeless, asking them if they knew the Sullivan brothers, Danny and Charlie. Of course they all said yes, but Pike hoped that one of them might really know the boys and have them contact him at his hotel.

When he got back to the hotel someone was again waiting for him in the lobby, but this time it was Joe Pitch.

"Where've you been all day?"

"Well, I spent a lot of time with the police," Pike said.

"I heard about that from Dundee."

"Where did he hear about it?"

"At the police station. What happened."

"Let's talk about it over a drink."

They went to the bar and took a table, and the bartender brought over two beers.

"Thanks, Lenny," Pitch said.

"Aren't you working here, any more?"

Pitch took a swallow of beer and said, "I took some

time off to work on your friend's case."

"Well, that's good to hear."

"Tell me what happened?"

Pike told Pitch about spotting the man who was following him and trying to sneak up on him.

"I like this," Pitch said.

"Like what?"

"The way this is going," Pitch said.

"What do you mean?"

"Listen," Pitch said, "who would have reason to follow you?"

"Someone sent by one of the fur companies, by Welles, or by whoever really killed Jennifer Welles."

"Right on all counts," Pitch said. "Now, suppose it was the real killer. What does that tell you?"

"It doesn't tell me anything."

"The two men in the tavern?"

"The two men in the—oh, I get it," Pike said. "You think that one of the men was following me, and that the other one killed him?"

"Right," Pitch said. "One partner killed the other partner."

"What for?"

"Who knows?" Pitch said. "Maybe one didn't want to split with the other."

"He's still got to split with the girl who drew McConnell out of the tavern."

"Not if he kills her, too."

"And maybe he already has," Pike said.

Pitch gave Pike a look of admiration and said, "Now that's very good."

"What do we do about it?"

"You do nothing," Pitch said. "You have to stay away from the police. They can't like you very much for finding that body."

"It wasn't my fault."

134

"The police are funny about placing blame where it doesn't belong," Pitch said. "That always seems to be the easy way out."

"So what are you gonna do, then?"

"I'm gonna check with the police and see if any dead girls have shown up over the past few days, besides Mrs. Welles."

"How do you suppose they got Jennifer Welles to that hotel room?" Pike asked.

"Was the man you found good-looking?"

Pike nodded and said, "I guess so, and young."

"Then that's how."

"How does a politician get involved with a woman like that?"

"Maybe she wasn't a woman like that when they met," Pitch suggested.

"Maybe," Pike said. "I've met Welles, he can't be too easy to live with."

"What about his sister?"

"What about her?"

"Is she still living with him?"

"The last I heard, yes."

Pike didn't know why, but he didn't tell Pitch that Lila was there at the hotel while his room was being searched, and he didn't tell him that the room had been searched. He preferred to keep those things to himself for the moment.

"What did you and Dundee do when I left this morning?" Pike asked.

"I nosed around, and he stuck his nose in his paperwork. I think he went to see McConnell tonight."

"That's good," Pike said. "They wouldn't let me see him. I don't want him thinking we forgot him."

"Nah," Pitch said. "Dundee will go and see him at least once a day until the trial."

"That's good."

"Tell me what else you've been doing?" Pitch said. "Get into any other trouble today?"

Pike told Pitch about visiting the fur companies.

"Well, that's a step in the right direction. What made you do that?"

"I promised Emerson I would," Pike said. "It was a condition of his letting me go."

"Well, I suppose he could have held you, but Dundee would have gotten you out."

"I've also been looking for the Sullivan brothers," Pike said.

"Who?"

"Didn't I tell you about them?"

"No, you didn't," Pitch said, "and if you did, I don't remember. Who are they?"

So Pike told Pitch about the two boys who tried to rob him.

"And you bought them dinner?" Pitch asked, laughing.

"What was I supposed to do?"

"I would have boxed their ears for them."

"And turned them over to the police?"

"No," Pitch said, "not that. I know what it's like to be homeless and hungry."

"You do?"

"Sure I do," Pitch said, "I wasn't always this rich—or this good-looking, for that matter. Sure, I lived on the streets for a while, before I started fighting for a living."

"For a living?" Pike said. "You mean you were a professional prize fighter?"

"You ever see a professional prize fight?"

"We had a fighter come to the mountains, once. Him and his manager were paying money to anyone who would go three rounds with him."

"And did anyone?"

"Nah," Pike said, "the kid was too fast, and too strong."

Pitch studied Pike's face and then said, "You're a liar."

"Wha—"

"You did it, didn't you? Come on, 'fess up. You went three rounds with him, didn't you?"

"No, I didn't," Pike said, into his beer.

"Why not?"

"He fell down after two."

"You knocked him out?"

"He was tired," Pike said. "He had gone three rounds with a few fellas, already."

"That's no excuse," Pitch said. "I've gone twenty or thirty rounds when I had to. You knocked him out, didn't you?"

"Yeah, well, I suppose I did."

"I knew it," Pitch said. "What was his name. Do you remember?"

"I don't know," Pike said, "Ray somebody."

"Ray somebody?" Pitch said, excitedly. "Ray McGregor? Was that it?"

"McGregor?" Pike said. "Yeah, that's it. Ray McGregor. That was his name."

"Oh, my God," Pitch said, "you knocked out Ray McGregor."

"You heard of him?"

"Heard of him," Pitch said. "My friend, Ray McGregor was only the champeen of the world for four years. For four years no one was able to touch him. I know, I tried and he knocked me out after twelve rounds."

"He was good, huh?"

"He was the best," Pitch said, in obvious admiration of the man, "and you knocked him out!"

137

"I was lucky," Pike said. "What was a man like that doing in the mountains, anyway?"

"I don't know," Pitch said, "all I know is that he and his manager disappeared after a fight in Chicago about six years ago."

"Disappeared? Where?"

"Well, you answered that. They were in the mountains for a while. They must have been hiding out."

"From what?"

"There was a group of men in Chicago who bet a lot of money that Ray would lose his title. He was *supposed* to lose his title. Not only did they bet a lot of money, they paid Ray's manager a lot of money."

"And?"

"And Ray knocked the bum out in two rounds."

"Those men must not have been happy."

"They would have killed him, and his manager, if they could have found him."

"Where is he now?"

"Who knows?" Pitch said. "Maybe he's in Europe. I hope he's over there. They really like prize fighting over there. Uh, you didn't hurt him or anything, did you?"

"No, he was back on his feet after a while."

"After a while?" Pitch said. "Come on, Pike, tell me about the fight."

"It wasn't much of a fight, Joe, believe me."

"But you knocked out Ray McGregor!"

"Look," Pike said, "maybe if we had gloves on—"

"You fought bare knuckled?"

"We had to," Pike said, "my hands were too big to fit the gloves they had."

"Oh, Jesus!" Pitch said, with feeling. "I wish I could have been there to see it. Oh Lord, that must have been something."

"It was okay—"

"Hey, Pike," Pitch said, "I got an idea."

"Why don't I like the tone of your voice?" Pike asked, warily.

"You're still young enough. Why don't you turn professional, and I'll manage you."

"No thanks."

"Pike, if you knocked out McGregor, you could be the champ in no time. The bum who's the champ now wouldn't stand a chance against you."

"What about you?"

"Me? I could probably knock him out, too—"

"Then why don't you fight him?"

"I'm retired."

"You're not that old."

"I'm old enough," Pitch said.

"Come on, Joe," Pike said, "why'd you retire when you obviously loved it so much?"

Suddenly, it was Pitch who didn't want to talk.

"Never mind," he said, standing up.

"Where are you going?"

"It's not too late for me to go to the police station to check and see if they had any dead girls the past few days."

"Hey, come on, Joe," Pike said, "finish your beer."

"I'll come by in the morning and let you know what I find out," Pitch said, and moved quickly to the exit.

"Jesus—" Pike said, confused.

The bartender, Lenny, came over to retrieve the empties and said, "Where's Joe goin' in such a hurry?"

"I don't know," Pike said, "we were talking about fighting, I asked him why he retired, and he got up and left."

"Oh," Lenny said, "that."

"What?"

"He didn't tell you?"

"Tell me what?"

139

"Maybe I shouldn't—"

"Lenny."

"He doesn't like to talk about his last fight."

"Why not?"

"They matched him with a kid, a good-looking kid, but still inexperienced."

"What happened?"

"Joe killed him."

"You mean he beat him bad?"

"No," Lenny said, "I mean he killed him. The kid went down in the fourteenth round, and he never got up. After that, Joe never fought again."

Now Pike understood.

"Thanks for telling me, Lenny."

"You won't tell Joe I said anything?"

"I won't tell."

"You want me to bring you another beer?"

"Definitely, Lenny," Pike said. "I think I need another beer."

When Pike returned to his room he paused in front of his door. There was light coming from beneath the door, and he did not recall leaving the lamp lit. He removed his Kentucky pistol from his belt and touched the doorknob. The door was unlocked, and he was sure he had locked it. He turned the knob, slammed the door open, and stepped into the room with the pistol held out in front of him.

"What the—" he said.

Irma, the blond whore, sat up in bed, holding the sheet in front of her, to cover herself.

"Oh," she said, relaxing, "it's you."

"What are you doing here?" he asked, lowering the pistol.

"Well," she said, "you didn't come looking for me, so

I came looking for you."

Pike was a little drunk.

"How did you get in here?" he demanded.

"Does that matter?"

Pike stared at her, and she very deliberately let the sheet drop, exposing her breasts. There was a smile on her face, and she wet her lips with her tongue.

"No," he said, reaching behind him to shut the door, "it doesn't matter at all."

CHAPTER SIXTEEN

Irma woke Pike the next morning the same way she had awakened him last time. He reached down to cup her head and closed his eyes, surrendering himself to the sensations she was causing with her talented tongue and mouth . . .

"Did I pay you last time?" Pike asked as Irma got dressed.

"In more ways than one, Pike," she said, smiling lasciviously.

"No, really . . ."

"You paid me."

Pike leaned over, reaching for his pants.

"What are you doing?" she asked.

"Getting my money so I can pay you."

She moved quickly to the bed, sat down next to him and pulled his pants out of his hands.

"I came to you, remember?" she asked.

"Yeah, but—"

"No buts, Pike," she said, leaning close to him. "This one was on the house. It was as much for me as it was for you."

She kissed him then, gently, her tongue tasting his lips.

As she walked to the door he called out, "Hey."

"What?"

"I don't know where to find you."

"That's all right," she said, "I know where to find you."

Pike dressed and went downstairs. He was at a loss as to what to do with himself and decided to go down the block to the cafe for breakfast. As he approached the cafe he thought he saw two figures out front that he recognized. As he got closer he was sure he recognized them.

Charlie and Danny Sullivan.

"Hello, boys."

"We got the word you was looking for us," Charlie said. "Why?"

"I hope it was to buy us another meal," Danny said.

His older brother whacked him in the ribs with his elbow.

"Well, if you boys can stand it, we can go inside and have breakfast."

"Is that what you wanted with us?" Charlie, the older asked.

"No," Pike said, "but we can discuss what I want over breakfast. What do you say?"

This time it was the younger brother who nudged the older with an elbow, and Charlie said, "Well, okay."

They went inside and Pike told the boys to order whatever they wanted. Both boys ordered steak and eggs, and cold milk. Pike ordered the same, and asked for some biscuits and butter, as well.

"So," Charlie Sullivan said around a mouthful of steak and eggs, "why were you looking for us?"

"I need your help."

"Our help?"

Pike nodded.

"What could we do for you?" Charlie asked, curiously. His tone said he thought the concept was unlikely.

"You fellas know the streets of St. Louis better than I do."

"Ha!" young Danny said. "Better than anybody!"

Charlie didn't say anything, but the look on his face said he agreed with his younger brother.

"I need for both of you to keep your ears open about the murder that happened the other day."

"The rich lady?" Charlie asked.

"That's right," Pike said. "You heard about it?"

"Sure, we did," Danny said. "Nothin' happens on the streets without us hearing about it."

Pike leaned forward and asked, "What do you know about it?"

"We know that a friend of yours was arrested for it," Danny said. "And we know that you hired Andy Dundee to defend him."

"You know Dundee, eh?"

"Sure," Charlie said, "us and Dundee are pals."

"Well, that's good," Pike said.

"Why?"

"He won't object when I tell him you're working for me."

"Working?" Charlie Sullivan asked.

"Yes," Pike said. "You know what the word 'work' means, don't you?"

"Hey, we ain't afraid of work," Danny said. "What I mean is, are you gonna pay us?"

"Of course," Pike said.

"How much?"

"A dollar a day."

144

"A dollar?" Charlie said. "That ain't hardly nothing!"

"It's more than you're making now," Pike said, "but there'll be more."

"When?" Danny asked. Charlie was too busy eating to answer questions. He was way ahead of his brother, and casting covetous glances at his brother's steak.

"Whenever you come up with something."

"About the murder?"

"That's right."

"Like the real killer?"

"That's right."

"That's supposin' there is another killer."

"There's not another killer, Danny," Pike said, "there's only one . . . the one who framed my friend, Skins McConnell."

"That's what you say."

"And I'll pay you even more," Pike said, "if you come up with something that helps me prove it."

"Anything?"

Pike narrowed his eyes at the young man and said, "Anything that's true. I don't want you making up a pack of lies on me."

"I wouldn't do that."

"Sure, you wouldn't."

"What do you say, Charlie?" Danny Sullivan asked his brother. "Should we work for Mr. Pike, here?"

"Sure, Danny," Charlie said. "We ain't got nothin' better to do."

"No," Danny said, "I guess we ain't."

"I want to know what anyone saw that day," Pike said. "Anyone around that hotel, or anyone around a tavern that's on . . . what the hell is the name of that street?"

"What street?"

"I was seeing somebody at the Hudson Bay Company, in a big building—"

"Hudson Bay?" Danny said. "I know where that is."

"Good. There's a tavern across the street where my friend was waiting for me. He met a woman, and they left together."

"The rich woman?" Charlie asked.

"No, not the rich woman," Pike said. "Another woman."

"Got a description of this woman?"

Pike dredged up the description the bartender in the tavern had given him and recited it.

"A woman who looks like that," Danny said, "someone must've seen her."

"Well, you find me that someone and I'll pay you handsomely."

Danny stood up and said, "We'll find you something, Pike."

"Are you gonna finish that steak?" Charlie asked his brother.

"Yeah, I am," Danny said. He took the steak from the plate, wrapped it up in a napkin and stuffed it inside his shirt. "Later."

Charlie wiped up the remnants of steak juice from his plate with a biscuit, shoved it in his mouth and stood up to leave with his brother.

"Danny?"

"Yeah?" Danny asked, turning back to the table.

Pike took out two dollars and handed it to him.

"What's this for?"

"Good faith."

Danny stared at Pike, then shrugged and put the money in his pocket. Pike was sure the boy didn't know what he was talking about.

"That's a dollar for you and a dollar for your brother, Danny."

"I handle the money in the family, Pike."

"I see."

"If we find out anything that you should know, we'll come to your hotel."

"That's fine," Pike said. "The trial is next Monday. I'd like to have something before then."

"If it's there," Danny said, "we'll find it."

"I hope so."

After the two boys left Pike finished his breakfast at a leisurely pace. He was back where he started that morning, unsure about what he should do.

Maybe he should go and talk to Dundee and see how McConnell was.

Healy pushed at the door and it swung open slowly. As he stepped through the doorway dust fell from the ceiling, almost choking him. This was not a part of town he usually frequented, but the man he wanted to talk to had chosen this as the meeting place. Because of what Richard Welles wanted, Healy had no choice but to accept.

He coughed, trying to clear the dust from his mouth and throat, and then advanced down the hallway.

"Key!" he called.

No answer.

"Ethan Key!"

"Back here."

The voice came from farther down the hall, and Healy moved toward it. When he came to the end of the hall he found himself in a dark room. The windows were boarded up, and slivers of light filtered in between the boards.

"Key?"

"I'm here."

"And Wayne?"

"I speak for Wayne," Key said. "We're partners."

"All right."

"You got a lot of nerve coming here . . . alone," Ethan Key said.

Healy still could not see the man. He did not reply to the man's comment, although he felt a secret surge of satisfaction at the man's words.

"I need something done, Key," Healy said. "You and your partner are the men to do it."

"Why should we?" Key asked. "Because you ask us to?"

"No," Healy said, "because it'll pay well."

"How well?"

"Very well."

"You're playing games, Healy."

"All right," Healy said. "A hundred dollars a man."

"To do what?"

"To kill a man."

There was a moment of silence and then Key's voice said, "Yeah . . . we could do that."

"Good. It has to be done soon."

"Soon as we get paid."

Healy put his hand in his pocket and came out with some money.

"Half now, and half when the job is done."

Again there was a few moments of silence while Key made up his mind.

"All right."

Healy held his hand out, and Key had to step forward to take the money. A couple of slivers of light illuminated his face for just a moment, and Healy saw the scars.

Only Ethan Key had scars on his face like that.

Key took the money and then moved back into the deep shadows.

"Wayne will go along with this?" Healy asked.

"He will."

148

"It's got to look like a robbery," Healy said, "or an accident. It's got to look like anything but what it is."

"A paid killing."

"Right."

"You know," Key said, "I find this odd."

"What?"

"That a policeman would pay me and Wayne to kill somebody."

"The money's not mine."

"It came from your hand."

"Only you and I know that, Key," Healy said, "and I'd deny it."

"I know you would."

"Do we have a deal?"

"We do," Key said. "We'll meet here after the job is done so you can pay me the rest of the money."

"Agreed."

"What's the man's name?"

"Pike," Healy said, "Jack Pike. He's staying at the Carlyle Hotel."

"Description?"

"You can't miss him," Healy said, and described Pike in detail.

"You're right," Key said, "I couldn't miss a man like that. Why do you want him dead?"

"Did I say I wanted him dead?" Healy said.

"Playing word games again, Healy?" Key asked. "You leave first, Lieutenant."

Healy nodded, backed out of the room, then turned and walked down the hall. He'd heard about Key's scars. But this was the closest he'd ever come to seeing them.

They said the scars on his face went even deeper than that, into his mind.

They said he was crazy.

And Healy had paid him to kill a man.

He wondered what that made him?

"Who is this Pike?" Cord Wayne asked.

Key poured himself a drink from the bottle they kept in the room and said, "I don't know."

"Did you ask?"

"No."

Wayne watched Key down the whiskey. The scars on Key's face were red and white, some of them crossing each other. One cheek almost had a checkerboard pattern. Wayne and Key had been partners for three years, and Wayne still had never had the nerve to ask Key how he got those scars.

Ethan Key was forty or so, although the scars made it hard to guess his age. He had black hair shot with gray. He didn't have a mustache or a beard because of the scars. He was tall, over six feet, and slender as a blade of grass, but Wayne knew how strong Key was. He had seen Key whip men twice his weight and girth.

Cord Wayne was thirty-eight, under six feet and thickset. Key was the one who killed with a gun, while Wayne killed with his hands, or with a knife.

"Well," Wayne said, "I guess it don't matter who he is or what he's done."

"It never has," Key said.

"It's just damn strange that it was Lieutenant Healy who hired us to do it."

"Strange," Key said, "but lucky. We'll have this over him, now and forever."

Wayne laughed.

"He thought you two were alone when he paid you," he said. "He thinks all he has to do is deny it, because it'd be his word against yours."

"He's got another think comin', hasn't he?" Ethan

Key said. "After we kill this Pike and get the rest of our money, we'll have Lieutenant Jerry Healy in our pockets for good."

"We could do a lot in this city with a policeman on our side."

"A policeman?" Key said. "Don't you know that Healy is an ambitious man? All we have to do is wait for him to get elected to some high office or other, and then we make our move."

"When are we gonna take care of this Pike?" Wayne asked.

"No time like the present," Ethan Key said, putting the cork back in the whiskey bottle. "Let's do it tonight."

Danny and Charlie Sullivan thought it was odd to see a policeman like Lieutenant Healy in one of the worst neighborhoods in St. Louis. Danny had had a few run-ins with Healy before he was a lieutenant, and knew that the man considered himself better than most.

"What's he doin' here?" Charlie asked.

"Let's find out," Danny said.

They followed Healy, and when the policeman had his meeting with Ethan Key, both boys were outside one of those boarded-up windows, listening.

After Healy left the boys watched and saw two men leave after him.

"That's Ethan Key, all right," Danny said.

"Which one?" Danny asked. He'd never seen Key, although he'd heard of him.

"The one with the scarred face."

"And the other one?"

"His partner, Cord Wayne."

"They really gonna kill Pike, Danny?"

"They been paid—half, at least," Danny said.

151

"They'll do it, all right."

"Do you think this something Pike would pay to know, Danny?"

Danny looked at his younger brother and smiled.

"Charlie, this is something Pike would pay a whole lot to know."

CHAPTER SEVENTEEN

The Sullivan brothers went to the Carlyle Hotel and entered the lobby. Immediately they attracted suspicious stares from guests and employees, alike. They approached the desk and the desk clerk sniffed audibly and glared at them.

"No begging in the lobby," he said.

Danny Sullivan bristled.

"We're not beggars!"

"Is that a fact?"

"We work for Mr. Pike."

"Who?"

"Jack Pike," Charlie said. "He's staying here."

"Pike?"

"A real big man with a beard?" Charlie said.

"Oh," the clerk said, "him." Again, he sniffed audibly, this one meant for Pike.

"Is he in his room?" Danny asked. "We got to talk to him."

"I wouldn't know."

"Did you see him leave?" Danny asked. "Or come in?"

"I'm sure I don't know."

Danny gave the clerk a baleful look, his version of

the clerk's disdainful sniff.

"People walk in and out of this hotel without you seeing them, mister?" he asked.

"Of course not."

"Then is Mr. Pike in or out?" Danny said.

"Check his box for his key, for Chrissake," Charlie said.

The clerk gave them both a glare, then turned and looked into Pike's box.

"His key is here," he finally admitted.

"He's out," Danny said, looking at his brother.

"We got to find him," Charlie said.

"Would you like to leave a message?"

Danny stared at the clerk. He would have liked to leave a message, all right, but neither he nor his brother knew how to write. He'd be damned if he'd tell the clerk that, though.

"No," he said, "that's all right. We'll find him and tell him ourselves. Come on, Charlie."

Charlie looked at the clerk and sniffed.

As the Sullivan boys were leaving the lobby Joe Pitch walked in. He saw them approaching him, and then passing him, and then turned.

"Hey!" he called.

Both boys stopped, shoulders hunched, ready to run. Danny turned and said, "We didn't do nothing."

"Are you the Sullivan boys?"

Danny gave the man a suspicious look and said, "Yeah, why?"

"I'm a friend of Pike's," Pitch said. "He mentioned he was looking for you boys."

"He found us," Danny said.

"He bought us breakfast," Charlie said, happily.

"What are you doin' back here now?"

"We were looking for Pike," Danny said. "We got something to tell him."

"He's not in?"

Both boys shook their heads.

"Well, then, you can tell me what you were gonna tell him."

The boys exchanged glances, and then Danny said, "No, we have to tell Pike."

"Was he gonna pay you?"

"Yes."

"I'll pay you."

Again they exchanged glances.

"Sorry," Danny said, "but we're working for Mr. Pike."

"Loyalty, huh?"

Both boys remained silent.

"You fellas know Andy Dundee?"

"Sure."

"I thought so," Pitch said. Dundee knew every street rat in St. Louis. "Well, he's working for Pike, too, and I'm working for Dundee."

"We still gotta tell Pike."

"Suppose we go to Dundee's office," Pitch said, "and you tell him?"

For the third time the brothers exchanged questioning glances.

"You trust Dundee, don't you?" Pitch asked.

"Of course," Danny said. Pitch knew they would. Dundee was one of them.

"Then let's go," Pitch said. "Whatever you wanted to tell Pike, you can tell Andy Dundee, right?"

Charlie looked at Danny, who nodded and said to Pitch, "All right."

Pitch nodded and said, "Let's go."

*　　　*　　　*

Pike, for want of something better to do, returned to the tavern across from the Hudson Bay office. As he walked in he took stock of the room, which was less than half occupied. He walked to the bar and the bartender grinned and wiped the bartop off with a wet towel.

"Beer?" he asked.

"Sure."

The bartender drew the cold beer and placed it before Pike.

"How are things going for your friend?"

"Not good," Pike said, picking up the beer.

"You come back to ask some more questions?"

Pike sipped the beer and lowered it.

"I thought you might have seen one of those two men again."

"No," the bartender said, "not since that day."

"Yeah," Pike said, "that's what I was afraid of. Thanks, anyway."

"Sure."

Pike picked up his beer and turned around, leaning against the bar. He saw a man at a back table who looked familiar, and then realized that it was Steven Stilwell, the man he had talked to from Hudson Bay. He groped for the man's title and then remembered that he was a president.

Pike took his beer and walked over to where Stilwell was sitting.

"Mr. Stilwell."

The man, who had been concentrating on destroying a bottle of whiskey, looked up. Half of the bottle was gone, and he squinted up at Pike, trying to place him.

"I know you?"

"Jack Pike. I was in your office a few days ago, talking about fur prices."

"Oh, that's right," Stilwell said, and returned his

gaze to the bottle. He picked it up and poured himself another glass.

Pike sat down across from him, but Stilwell did not seem to notice.

"I wonder if you had a chance to think over what we talked about," Pike said.

Stilwell looked across the table at Pike, as if surprised to find him sitting there.

"What was that?"

"About fur prices?" Pike said. "The possibility of Hudson Bay raising their prices to the trappers?"

"Oh," Stilwell said, "that." The look on his face, and his attitude, said that fur prices were the farthest thing from his mind.

"Have I caught you at a bad time?" Pike asked.

The man looked at him and said, "Yes, you have caught me at a decidedly bad time."

The first time Pike had met the man, in his office, Stilwell had been neatly dressed, clean-shaven and clear-eyed. The man sitting across from him now was disheveled, was carrying around a two-day growth of beard, and had red-rimmed eyes behind his wire frame glasses.

"I'm sorry," Pike said. "I hope it isn't something . . . serious."

Stilwell smiled, a small, ironic smile.

"It's as serious as it can get, Mr. Pike," he said. "Death always is."

"Death?"

Stilwell nodded.

"Someone close to me."

"Was it sudden?"

"Very sudden."

"I'm sorry," Pike said. "I'll leave you to your grief, then."

Pike stood up.

"Mr. Pike," Stilwell said, grabbing for the bottle. He misjudged the distance and knocked it over, but Pike caught it before it could hit the table and spill. "Thank you. Uh, Mr. Pike, perhaps we can talk about fur prices another time, in a few days."

"Maybe we can, Mr. Stilwell."

Pike went back to the bar, paid for his beer and left the empty mug.

"Comin' back?" the bartender asked.

"I don't think so," Pike said. "If you happen to see one of those men, I'm at the Carlyle Hotel."

"I'll send a message."

Pike started for the door.

"Hey, fella!" the bartender called.

Pike turned.

"Yeah?"

"I haven't seen those two men," the man said, "but I did see that woman again."

"You did?"

Pike went back to the bar. In the mirror behind it he could see Steve Stilwell passing behind him on the way out of the place.

"When did you see her?" Pike asked, leaning his elbows on the bar excitedly.

"Last night."

"Here?"

"Yep."

"Are you sure it was her?"

"Positive," the man said. "I wouldn't forget a gal like that."

"Was she with anyone?"

"She sure was," the bartender said. "That fella who just left here."

Pike turned and looked behind him.

"Which fella?"

"The one who just walked out the door," the

bartender said. "Sort of short, thin fella in need of a shave? You were sitting with him a minute ago."

"Stilwell?" Pike said, in surprise. "She was sitting with Stilwell?"

"Is that his name?" the man said. "All I know is he works across the street. Comes in here sometimes for lunch, sometimes after work. Last night he was here after work, and she was sitting with him—hey, where you going—"

Pike didn't answer. He was already out the door and running across the street to the building where Hudson Bay had their offices.

As Pike burst into the offices of Hudson Bay the woman seated behind the reception desk stared at him in horror. She remembered him from the last time he was there, and he was easily the largest man she had ever seen in all her twenty-three years. She had looked at him then with a mixture of awe and horror. Now there was just horror in her face.

"Where is Stilwell?" he demanded.

"M-M-Mr. Stilwell is not here, sir."

Pike approached the desk and loomed menacingly over her, although it was not his intention to menace her in any way.

"I just saw him across the street, and he left before me."

"He didn't come back here, sir," she said, "I can assure you."

"Damn!" he said, frightening her even more with his vehemence, even though it was not directed at her. "What's his address?"

"Sir," she said, her voice a squeak, "I can't give you that information. Is there someone else in the company who could help you?"

"Little lady," Pike said leaning on the desk, "I have to see Stilwell, and I have to see him now. Where does he live?"

"Sir, I could get fired—"

He looked behind her at the file cabinets.

"Which of those things is his address in?"

"Sir—"

"I'm not asking you for his address, miss," Pike said, "just where it is. I'll look it up myself. They can't pay you enough to try to stop me from doing that, can they?"

"N-no, sir," she said. She turned and pointed to the center cabinet. "T-That one."

He went around the desk and she stood up and scooted out of his way.

There were three drawers in the cabinet and he turned and looked at her again.

"T-top one. It has all our personnel files."

Pike didn't know what a personnel file was, but he opened the drawer and started leafing through folders until he found one with the name "Stilwell" on it. He pulled it out, opened it and read the address, memorizing it, then returned the file neatly.

He turned to the girl, who cowered against the wall.

"I'm sorry, miss," he said, "I didn't mean to scare you, but this is important."

"Y-you're not going to h-hurt him, or anything, are you?" she asked.

"No," he said, "I just want to ask him one question."

As he left he was thinking that whether or not Stilwell got hurt depended on his answer to that question. Skins McConnell was running out of time, and Pike was tired of waiting for something to happen.

He was going to start making things happen.

PART FIVE

COINCIDENCE

CHAPTER EIGHTEEN

Andy Dundee looked up as the door to his office opened and he saw the Sullivan boys enter.

"What brings you boys here?" he asked, sitting back in his broken chair.

"He does," Danny said, jerking his thumb behind him. Joe Pitch entered behind the two boys.

"Joe, what's going on?" Dundee asked.

"These two boys were at the hotel looking for Jack Pike, but he wasn't there," Pitch said. "Apparently they're working for him, and have something to tell him."

"Is that a fact, boys?"

"That's right," Danny said. "He was gonna pay us for information."

"About what?"

"About the rich lady who got killed?" Charlie Sullivan said.

"And you have some information?" Dundee asked.

"Not about the lady," Danny said.

"About what, then?"

"About Pike," Charlie said.

Dundee stared at them and said, "You boys gonna make us drag this out of you, or are you gonna tell us what the hell you're talking about?"

"You gonna pay us?" Danny Sullivan asked.

"If the information is worth anything."

"Oh, it's worth something, all right," Danny said.

"All right, then," Dundee said, "tell us."

"You know Ethan Key?"

Dundee's eyebrows shot up.

"Sure, I know about Key," Dundee said. "He's a killer for hire, him and his partner, Cord Wayne. What about them, boys?"

Danny and Charlie Sullivan exchanged glances, and then Danny looked at Dundee and said, "They been hired to kill Pike."

Pitch made a noise behind them and Dundee sat up straight in his chair.

"Are you sure about this, boys?" Dundee asked.

"We was there," Danny said, "outside the building, listening."

"And they were hired to kill Pike?"

"That's right."

"When did this happen?"

"Just today."

"And who did the hiring?"

"Is this worth money?"

"It's worth money," Dundee said, nodding. "Who did the hiring?"

The boys looked at each other and fidgeted.

"You may not believe us," Danny said.

"I'll believe you."

"And you'll pay us?"

"I'll pay you," Dundee said. He reached for his jacket and took his wallet from the inside pocket. "Now who did the hiring?"

Danny Sullivan took a deep breath and said, "Healy."

Dundee stared at him, and then said, "I don't believe it."

"See—" Danny started.

"Lieutenant Jerry Healy?" Dundee said.

"That's right."

"You know Healy?"

"Yeah, we do," Danny said. He felt now that Dundee wasn't going to pay them because he didn't believe them. They should have gotten some money in advance.

"And you're sure it was him?"

"We saw them," Danny said, impatiently. "Healy, Ethan Key, and Cord Wayne."

"And Healy talked to them?"

"Healy talked to Key," Danny said. "He didn't see the other man."

Dundee looked past the boys at Pitch, who raised his eyebrows and whistled soundlessly.

"Boys," Dundee said, taking a few bills from his wallet, "I need you to do me a favor."

"A favor?" Danny asked.

"It's a favor I'll pay you for," Dundee said. He picked up the bills and handed them to Danny, who clutched them greedily.

"That's for the information," Dundee said. "Now comes the favor."

"What is it?"

"Find Jack Pike," Dundee said. "We've got to find Pike and warn him. Can you do that for me? Can you do that for Pike?"

"We can do that," Danny said. Having learned his lesson he said, "You gonna pay us something now?"

Dundee took out another bill and passed it to him.

"I'll match that if you locate Pike."

"We'll find him," Danny said. "Come on, Charlie."

165

They moved past Pitch to the door, then Danny turned and asked, "If we find him, and he gets killed anyway, do we still get paid?"

Dundee stared at them and said, "You'll still get paid."

After the two boys left, Dundee said, "Mercenary little bastards, aren't they?"

"Healy hiring Key and Wayne?" Pitch said, shaking his head. "Does that make sense to you?"

"Sure," Dundee said, "doesn't it make sense to you?"

"No," Pitch said. "I don't understand why a police lieutenant would be paying two killers."

"Paying them?" Dundee said, standing up and grabbing his jacket. "He's not paying them, Joe, he's hiring them."

"Then who's paying them?"

"Who does Healy see as his ticket into politics?" Dundee asked.

"Richard Welles?"

"That's right."

"Andy," Pitch said, "this isn't just your way of going after Welles, is it?"

"Think about it, Joe," Dundee said, "and it'll make sense to you. Now let's get going."

"To the police?"

Dundee shook his head.

"We don't have time to go to the police and try to convince them," he said. "We've got to find Pike, and we've got to find him fast. If we don't he could be dead by nightfall."

Pike grabbed a buggy outside of the Hudson Bay building and gave the man Steven Stilwell's address. When they arrived Pike saw that it was a residential area, and although the homes were not as fancy looking and expensive as Richard Welles's, they were certainly impressive.

He paid the driver, went to the front door and banged on it. It was opened by a plain-looking woman in an even plainer dress, a puzzled look on her face. She appeared to be in her thirties, but she was so thin Pike could see the points of her shoulders and wristbones.

"Can I help you?"

"Does Steve Stilwell live here?"

"He does," she said. "I'm Mrs. Stilwell."

Pike could see why Stilwell might have been sitting in a bar last night with a beautiful woman.

"I'd like to talk to him."

"Steven is not home," she said. "He's at work."

Pike started to say that he wasn't, then decided not to alarm the woman. He believed her when she said he wasn't home, or he might have bulled past her to take a look. She probably had enough surprises coming to her, though.

"I'll try him there, then," Pike said.

"Is there something I can help you with, mister . . . ?"

"No, I don't think so, Mrs. Stilwell," Pike said. "I'll discuss it with your husband, when I find him."

"Well, he should be at his office."

He should be, Pike thought, but he's not. He wondered if Stilwell was with the other woman right now.

He started down the steps, then stopped and turned to face the plain woman again.

"Mrs. Stilwell, if your husband wasn't at work now, where would he be?"

"Why wouldn't he be at work?" she asked, frowning. The concept looked totally unbelievable to her. If her husband wasn't at work, he was home, and that was that.

"I'd just like to know where else I could look for him,

if he wasn't there," Pike said. "A favorite place, or a restaurant?"

"Not that I know of," she said.

"All right, Mrs. Stilwell," he said. "Thank you kindly."

He went down the stairs and she closed the door behind him.

Where the hell was Steve Stilwell?

"Steve," Karen Akers said, backing away from her door in surprise, "what are you doing here?"

"I had to see you, Karen," a panic-stricken Steven Stilwell told the beautiful young woman in front of him. "Can I come in . . . please?"

"Of course, darling," Karen said, "of course you can come in."

Stilwell squeezed past her into her rooms and she closed the door behind him.

"Can I get you a drink?" she asked.

"No," he said, shaking his head, "no, I've had too much to drink already. My God, Karen—"

"What's wrong, Steve?" she asked, solicitously. "Can you tell me?"

"Jennifer—" he said, choking on the name. "Who killed her, Karen?"

"Well, how would I know that, silly?"

"You asked me to have her meet me at that hotel," Stilwell said, "and now she's dead. Are you telling me you don't know anything about that?"

"Of course I don't, darling," she said, "why would I? Here, let me make you a drink. Come over here."

She put her hand on his arm, maneuvering him around so that his back was to the door of the other room. As she poured him a drink, the connecting door opened and a man crept from the room. He moved in behind Stilwell and very quickly grasped the man's head and twisted it. The sound of his neck snapping was like a dry twig and Karen Akers gasped.

"Did you have to do that?" she demanded.

"What do you think?" Leonard Roberts asked her.

"I think," she said, "that I never should have gotten involved in this mess."

"Well, you are involved," Leonard Roberts said. "You're the one who picked this sap to use as the bait."

"Well, you're the one who picked a mountain man as a patsy," she said. "Which one of us is the dumber."

Before she could move he slapped her across the face hard enough to leave the imprint of his hand on her fair skin.

"You are," he said, "for talking to me like that."

Rubbing her cheek, tears stinging her eyes she said, "I'm sorry."

"I know you are," he said. He reached for her and she cringed, but he only took her in his arms. "I have to get rid of the body."

"Why don't we leave this town, Leonard?" she asked.

"We will, baby," he said, rubbing her back, "as soon as I get my money."

She almost said, "our money," but she didn't want to get slapped again.

Pike went back to the Hudson Bay office, but Steven Stilwell had not returned. He left, not wishing to terrorize the poor receptionist any further.

He decided to go back to the hotel.

Cord Wayne's part in the partnership with Ethan Key was usually spotting the victim. Key couldn't very well have stood across the street from the Carlyle

169

Hotel, waiting for Pike to arrive. His scars would have attracted too much attention. It was up to Wayne to wait there, matching the description they had with everyone who came and went from the hotel.

When he saw the tall, bearded man walking down the street with long-legged strides, he knew that this was Jack Pike. Jesus, he thought, look at the size of that buck!

Pike entered the hotel and Wayne left the doorway. They had taken a room nearby, where Ethan Key was waiting for Wayne to come and get him once he spotted Pike.

Now that Pike was in the hotel, he'd be easy prey for Ethan Key and Cord Wayne.

CHAPTER NINETEEN

The Sullivan boys had looked all over the city for Pike and, not finding him, decided to go back to his hotel to see if he had returned.

Pitch and Dundee had checked the tavern where McConnell had been waiting for Pike, and found out from the bartender that Pike had been there. The bartender told them that he had seen the woman who had taken McConnell out of there, and had told Pike that. When he described the man whom Pike had been sitting with at the bar, neither Pitch nor Dundee recognized the description. Also, neither of them remembered that Hudson Bay was across the street.

They decided to go back to Pike's hotel and see if he had returned.

When Pike approached the front desk to ask for his key the clerk sniffed.

"You got a cold?"

"You should tell your young friends not to clutter up the lobby," the clerk said.

"Give me my key," Pike said. Accepting it he asked, "What young friends?"

171

"The two vagabonds who were here earlier."

"Vagabonds?"

"Street urchins."

"Talk English, man."

"The two filthy young boys who were looking for you," the clerk said, impatiently.

The Sullivans.

"When were they here?" he asked.

"Earlier."

"How much earlier?"

"Hours."

"Did they say what they wanted?"

"Only that they wanted to talk to you."

"Did they leave a message?"

"No," the clerk said, "but they left here with your friend."

"What friend?"

"The bartender from the bar, here," the clerk said. "What's his name?"

"Joe Pitch."

"That's him."

Pike thought for a moment. If they had something to tell him, maybe Pitch had taken them to tell Dundee.

"Here," he said, handing the key back, "I changed my mind."

The clerk took the key back and sniffed.

Pike turned and started from the hotel.

Across the street from the hotel Cord Wayne had returned to his doorway. He did not know that it was the same doorway in which Robert Cole had recently lost his life. If he had, he might have taken it as a bad sign and chosen another doorway.

*   *   *

172

Across the street, on the same side as the hotel, Ethan Key stood. He was in the doorway of a locked hotel side door. If anyone passing by had bothered, they could have looked at him and seen his scars. For the most part people walked by without glancing at him. For those who did, he kept his hat down over his eyes and ignored them.

Danny and Charlie Sullivan were running down the street toward the hotel when Danny grabbed Charlie's arm.

"Look," he said. He was pointing to a doorway across the street, where a man was standing, obviously watching the hotel.

"Who is it?" Charlie asked.

"That looks like Cord Wayne," Danny said. He looked around and said, "Key has to be around here somewhere."

"They're waiting for Pike!" Charlie said.

"Yeah," Danny said, "we gotta warn him. Come on."

They started running toward the hotel.

A buggy pulled up in front of the hotel just as Pike came out the door. From the buggy stepped Joe Pitch and Andy Dundee. They saw Pike at the same time he saw them. Pike was disappointed that the Sullivan boys were not with them.

"Hey," he said.

"Hey!" Pitch called out.

"Hey! Hey!" someone else was shouting.

Pike started walking toward Pitch and Dundee when he heard the "Hey, hey!" that someone was calling. He looked to his left and saw the Sullivan boys running toward him, waving their arms.

Ethan Key stepped from his doorway as Pike came through the door. At the same moment Cord Wayne stepped from his and started across the street.

In the same moment, the buggy pulled up in front of the hotel. Two men stepped from it, and two boys were running down the street shouting.

Key knew immediately that it had gone bad, but he and Wayne were caught out in the open.

Key pulled his pistol from his belt.

"Danny!" Pike called, turning toward the boys. With that move he gave Ethan Key his back.

"Pike, look out!" Danny shouted.

Pitch, watching Pike, turned his head to his left in time to see Ethan Key aiming his pistol at Pike.

"Pike! Behind you!"

Pike turned at the warning from Pitch. He saw Key aiming his pistol and immediately dropped to his knees. He heard the shot and saw the muzzle flash as he pulled his own pistol from his belt. He didn't know where Key's ball had gone, but he aimed and put his right where he wanted to—in Ethan Key's heart.

Cord Wayne knew that there was no way to stop things now. He took out his knife as Ethan Key fired, and continued to run across the street.

Dundee heard the sound of footsteps behind them and turned. He saw a man running toward them, brandishing a knife. He didn't know exactly who the man was headed for, and he didn't care.

"Joe!" he called.

Joe Pitch heard Dundee call and turned in time to

174

see the man coming around the buggy. He stepped in front of the man to intercept him. The man stopped, then jabbed at Pitch with the knife. Pitch feinted right, moved left and hit the man with a picture-perfect right cross. The man went down as if he had been poleaxed.

Pike stood up as Ethan Key fell and looked at Pitch in time to see him throw the punch.

"Mr. Pike!" he heard someone yell from behind him.

It was Charlie Sullivan, who was crouched over his brother's prone figure.

Now Pike knew where Ethan Key's ball had gone.

He turned and shouted to Pitch, "Hold that buggy."

He rushed to Danny Sullivan's side. If he was still alive they'd need the buggy to take him to a doctor.

The buggy driver, who when all this had started had thrown himself beneath his buggy, came out now, surveyed the scene and said, "Sweet Jesus!"

CHAPTER TWENTY

Pike sat across from Inspector Earl Emerson and waited for the man to speak again. He had been in the office for the better part of a half an hour, and wanted to get out and get to the hospital to check on Danny Sullivan's condition.

"I can't believe this," Emerson finally said.

"You don't want to believe it," Pike said.

"I'm supposed to take the word of a . . . a street rat that a policeman hired two killers?"

"Two street rats," Pike said.

"If the older boy lives and tells the same story," Emerson said.

"Well, why don't we get out of here and see how he's doing?"

"Not yet," Emerson said, "I'm not done, yet. This time, you have killed someone, Pike. You're not going to walk away that easy."

"Yes," Pike said, "I am."

"What?"

"I don't deny killing the man, Inspector, but I've got witnesses who say that he fired first—and one of them is my lawyer."

"Andy Dundee," Emerson said, "don't remind me."

"The fact of the matter is, two men tried to kill me," Pike said. "I killed one, and Joe Pitch caught the other one. What does he have to say?"

"Nothing."

"Well, let me talk to him for a while," Pike said, "I'll get him to say something, I guarantee you that."

"We'll take care of that, Pike," Emerson said.

"Why don't you question Richard Welles?"

"What for?"

"Because maybe he hired those two to kill me."

"You just finished telling me Lieutenant Healy hired them."

Pike had had a chance to discuss this with Dundee and Pitch, and he agreed with Dundee's theory, which he now tried to give to Emerson.

"You know how Healy feels about Richard Welles, Emerson," Pike said. "If Welles said that he wanted me out of the way, and he wanted Healy to handle it, what would Healy do?"

"I don't—"

"Would he kill me himself?"

Emerson snorted and said, "He wouldn't have the nerve to."

"So then he'd hire it done," Pike said. "He's in a good position to know who to hire, isn't he?"

"So am I."

"But you didn't do it," Pike said, "he did—and I think you know that."

"Knowing and proving are two different things."

"Then let's prove it."

"How?"

"Let me out of here."

"What good will that do?"

"Healy's men have failed. If Welles still wants me out of the way, he'll try again. Maybe this time he'll try it himself."

177

"If he does that . . ." Emerson said.

"You'll be there to catch him."

Emerson thought that over, and Pike was hoping that he had won the policeman over. He was becoming more and more anxious about Danny's condition—and not to be lost in the confusion was Skins McConnell's problem.

Maybe if Welles was behind the attempt on Pike, he was also behind his wife's death.

"What do you say, Inspector?"

Emerson looked at Pike and said, "Let's go and see how the boy is doing."

When they arrived at the hospital Joe Pitch was sitting on a bench with young Charlie Sullivan. Andy Dundee was leaning against the wall, and saw Pike and Emerson.

"Didn't need me to get out, I see," Dundee said.

"The inspector has been very understanding," Pike said. "How is Danny?"

"We don't know, yet," Dundee said. "They're still working on him."

"I'll talk to the other boy again," Emerson said.

"Take it easy on him," Pike said. "He's waiting for his brother to live or die."

"Don't worry," Emerson said, and walked over to where Pitch and Charlie Sullivan were seated.

"What happened?" Dundee asked.

"He doesn't want to believe it about Healy, but I think he does," Pike said. He relayed his conversation with Emerson to Dundee, who nodded.

"So you'll walk the streets waiting for Healy, or someone else hired by him, to try to kill you again?" he asked when Pike finished.

"Well, I'm not just going to wander the streets."

"What do you plan to do?"

"I'm going to push Richard Welles a little."

"How?"

"Through his sister."

"His sister?"

"That's right."

"What are you talking about?"

"I'm talking about his sister, Lila."

"Listen," Andy Dundee said, "I've made it my business to know all there is to know about this man."

"So?"

"So," Dundee said, "he doesn't have a sister."

"What?"

"Read my lips," Andy Dundee said, "Richard Welles does not have a sister. He was an only child."

"What about . . . a half sister?"

"His parents are both dead," Dundee said. "They died when he was young. He has no living relatives."

"Then who's the woman staying in his house with him?" Pike asked.

"I don't know," Dundee said. "Why don't you ask Inspector Emerson? Maybe he'd be interested in knowing that a man whose wife has just been killed a few days ago has a woman staying in his house with him."

"No," Pike said, "before I talk to Emerson, I think I'll go and talk to the lady herself."

"Well, go on, then," Dundee said. "We'll keep the inspector busy here. Healy doesn't know what's happened yet, so you should be safe on the streets."

As Pike left the hospital Dundee added to himself, "For a while, anyway."

Pike waved down a buggy outside and gave the driver Richard Welles's address. This time he was hoping that Welles would not be home. He wanted to talk to Lila—if that was her name—alone.

He knocked on the door, and when there was no answer he tried the doorknob. It turned, and the door swung open.

Cautiously, he stepped inside. The house sounded quiet—too quiet.

He removed the reloaded Kentucky pistol from his belt and moved farther into the house. When he reached the living room he saw that the furniture had been overturned, obviously the result of some sort of struggle.

Puzzled, he continued to look around the house. When he finished with the first floor, he went up the stairs to the second floor.

He found the body in the bedroom where he and Lila had made love.

He knew Inspector Emerson was really not going to be happy with him.

Hours had passed by the time Pike returned to the hospital, fetched Emerson and returned to the house with him and some of his men.

"The living room was like this when you got here?" Emerson asked.

"That's right."

"Where is the body?" Emerson asked.

"Upstairs in the master bedroom."

"Stay here," the inspector told Pike. He turned to two of his men and said, "Make sure he stays here."

"Yes, sir."

To the third man he said, "Come with me."

Pike waited while Emerson and his man went upstairs. He was thinking how funny it would be if Emerson came down and said there was no body. From what Pike could see, the cause of death had been a broken neck, so there would be no telltale bloodstains. If the body was gone, he was going to look like a real fool.

He waited with the two policemen, each of whom were staring at him, not taking their eyes off him. Pike found other things to look at while waiting.

Upon his return to the hospital he discovered that Danny Sullivan had survived his surgery. Now the doctors were waiting for his body to make its decision—live or die. It was up to him.

Finally, Emerson came back down, without his man.

"Do you know who she was?" Emerson asked.

"She said her name was Lila Welles," Pike said. "She claimed to be Richard Welles's sister."

"Claimed?"

"Dundee says that Welles doesn't have a sister," Pike said. "Do you know if that's true?"

"Not for sure," Emerson said, "but it shouldn't be too hard to find out."

"So what do we do now?"

Emerson stared at Pike and asked, "Did you kill her, Pike?"

"No, Inspector, I did not."

"Do you think Healy had this done, too?" Emerson asked, and then walked away from him before he could answer. The other two policemen exchanged glances, but said nothing.

"Damn it!" Emerson said. "This is the second body we've found today with its neck broken."

"What was the other one?" Pike asked.

"A man," Emerson said. "He was found in an alley— wiat a minute." Emerson turned and looked at Pike. "Do you believe in coincidence?"

"Not really," Pike said. "I think everything happens for a purpose. Why?"

"The dead man's name was Steven Stilwell," Emerson said. "He worked at the Hudson Bay company. Did you know him?"

"Jesus," Pike said. "Yeah, I knew him. I've been looking for him."

"Well," Emerson said, "since neither one of us believes in coincidence, suppose you convince me that you didn't find him."

PART SIX

POINTS OF VIEW

CHAPTER TWENTY-ONE

"Look at it from my point of view," Inspector Emerson said.

"I'm trying to," Pike said. "See, my problem is, I know I haven't done anything."

"Well, I don't have that problem," Emerson said. "I have to go by the facts that I see."

"And what are they?" Pike asked.

"There's a dead girl upstairs, and a dead man in an alley," Emerson said. "Both have broken necks, both have a connection to you. Mrs. Welles is dead, and the man arrested for that murder is connected to you. You are connected to an awful lot of murders for someone as innocent as you claim to be."

"What about the fact that someone tried to kill me? What does that tell you?"

"That tells me that a man involved in so many deaths might have made someone mad enough to want to kill him," Emerson said. "What does it tell you?"

"It tells me I've gone and gotten myself into something I may have a hard time getting myself out of," Pike said. "If someone doesn't kill me, you'll lock me up for killing someone."

"It does look kind of hopeless, doesn't it?" Emerson said.

"And what about for my friend, McConnell?"

"Well," Emerson said, "your situation may be starting to look more hopeless than his."

"Oh? How's that?"

"A second death having to do with Richard Welles? And we've had your friend in jail for days. There has to be a connection, and if there is, he's in the clear."

"Well," Pike said, "good for him. Now let's talk about me again."

"All right," Emerson said. "Tell me more about the dead girl."

"What can I tell you?" Pike said. "She claimed she was Welles's sister."

"When?"

"The first time I met her, right here in this house. I came to see Welles the day after his wife was killed. Lila—that's what she said her name was—opened the door, introduced herself as Lila Welles, and invited me in."

"She was a good-looking woman," Emerson said.

"I noticed that, too," Pike said, ignoring Emerson's insinuation.

"What did she tell you?"

"That Welles was not here. She didn't seem too upset over the fact that his wife had been killed. She said that she had come here to be with him because, whatever she felt about him or his wife, he was the only family she had."

"What else?"

"She came to my hotel the next day, kept me busy in the dining room while someone went through my room."

"For what?"

"I don't know."

Emerson gave him a suspicious stare.

186

"Look, don't go getting suspicious over nothing," Pike said. "I didn't have anything in my room that anyone would want."

"All right," Emerson said. "Tell me about Steven Stilwell."

"I met him when I went to Hudson Bay to talk to them about raising their price on furs."

"And he's the man you spoke to?"

"Yes."

"And then?"

"I didn't see him again until yesterday, at that tavern across from his office. He was a different man."

"How do you mean?"

"He'd been drinking heavily, he hadn't shaved, his eyes were red, either from drinking or from crying."

"Crying?"

"He was talking about death, as if he had lost someone close to him."

"Like who?"

"Like maybe . . . Jennifer Welles?"

"You think he was one of her lovers?"

"That's what I think."

"Did you ask him about her?"

"No, I didn't connect them at the time."

"When did you connect them?"

"Not until Stilwell left the bar," Pike said. "That's when the bartender told me that he had seen Stilwell with the girl who took McConnell out of the bar."

"When?"

"The night before. I went looking for Stilwell. I checked his office, his home, and his office again. I never found him." Pike leaned closer to Emerson and repeated, "I never found him."

Emerson stared at Pike and scratched his nose.

"You gonna lock me up, Inspector?"

Emerson hesitated a few moments, then said, "No, I'm not. My police instincts tell me to put you away for a while."

"But?"

"My gut tell me to let you run a little."

"As bait.",

"It was your idea first, remember?"

"I remember," Pike said, "and I still think it's a good one."

"All right," Emerson said. "I'm going from here to Welles's office, to question him about this. After that, he's all yours."

"What about Healy?" Pike asked. "What are you gonna do about him?"

"Nothing, for a while," Emerson said. "I'm gonna give you a chance to get me all the proof I need against him, too."

"You're taking a big chance with me, Inspector," Pike said. "Why?"

"I told you," Emerson said. He touched his stomach and said, "I'm going by what's in here. I've got a lot of bodies, and a lot of coincidence, but no case. I have a feeling if I leave you on the loose, it might all become tied together."

"It won't all just become tied together, Inspector," Pike said. "I'm gonna tie it together for you."

"You do that, mountain man," Emerson said, "and I just might offer you a job as a detective."

"I think I'll stick to the mountains, but thanks just the same."

"That's the other side of the coin."

"What do you mean?"

"I mean," Emerson said, moving closer to Pike, "if you don't find me someone else to hang all of this on, you may never see your mountains again."

Pike took a few moments to find his voice and then

said, "I'll keep that in mind."

Being threatened with the loss of his beautiful mountains was a sobering thought for Pike, so after hearing it, he needed a drink.

He went back to his hotel and into the bar. He got a beer from the bar and took it to a table, and then sat staring into it. It was as if he thought that a picture would form there, showing him what he needed to know.

He was killing time, waiting for Emerson to finish with Welles so that he could go and see him afterward. Emerson had said he'd try to get Welles to go back to his house, and that Pike should try there first.

Who had he met in the past few days who would have a motive to kill him?

Certainly not Andy Dundee or Joe Pitch. What he'd done was give them work. They wouldn't want to kill him for that, would they?

What about the Sullivans? They were just boys, and one of them had been wounded in the attempt.

Stilwell? Could he have hired someone to kill Pike before he was killed himself?

And what about "Lila Welles," if that was even her name? Could she have done that?

Pike's best guess was Richard Welles. He was a politician, a breed of man Pike was not used to dealing with. From what he had heard, however, such men were not beyond killing to get what they want, or to keep what they have.

In fact, Welles could even be behind all three deaths—his wife's, Stilwell's and Lila's.

In *fact,* there was as much coincidence involved with Welles as there was with Pike—maybe even more.

Pike certainly hoped that Inspector Emerson was

going to threaten Welles with the equivalent to threatening *him* with the loss of his mountains.

Jerry Healy was worried.

It was obvious by now that Key and Wayne had failed to kill Pike. If they had, he would have heard from them by this time.

The fact that he had not heard from them by now could mean that Pike had killed one or both of them. It could also mean that Key and Wayne had not made their attempt yet, but Healy didn't believe that for a minute. He had impressed upon Key the urgency of the matter, and he was sure the two men would have made their attempt by now.

If they had tried, and had failed, why had he not heard about it by now? Emerson surely would have brought Pike in for questioning if he had been directly involved in a killing.

Healy had a bad feeling that someone was keeping something from him.

It was time to go and see Richard Welles.

"I don't understand," Welles said to Emerson.

"It's very simple, Mr. Welles," Emerson said. "A woman was killed in your house. Do you know who she is?"

Welles leaned back in his chair, regarding Emerson from behind his desk.

"I don't keep women at my house, Inspector," he said, "especially not immediately following my wife's death."

"Murder," Emerson said, "your wife's murder."

"Yes, I know my wife was murdered."

"Well, so was this woman," Emerson said. "Her neck

was broken. Did you know her?"

"How do I know if I know her if I haven't seen her?" Welles asked.

"Well, this might help," Emerson said. "She claimed to be your sister."

"My sister?" Welles said. He laughed and added, "Inspector, I do not have a sister."

"Then what was this woman doing in your house?"

"I've told you," Welles said, growing agitated now, "I haven't had a woman in my house."

"Well, there was one there today," Emerson said, "and she was dead. If you'd be so kind, I'd like you to come down to the undertaker's to take a look at the body."

"Of course," Welles said. "Tell me, was my house broken into?"

"No, it wasn't."

"That's odd," Welles said. "How did she get in there, then?"

"Well, Mrs. Welles," Emerson said, "we don't exactly know that."

"How did you know she was there?"

"A man found her."

"What man?"

"His name is Pike," Emerson said. "I believe you know him?"

"We've met," Welles said. "What was he doing there?"

"Looking for you, apparently."

"Well, do you have him in custody?"

"No, we don't."

"Why not?" Welles demanded. "Isn't he a suspect?"

"He's as much a suspect as you are, Mr. Welles," Emerson said. "If you please, I'd like to see you at the undertaker's within the next two hours."

"I will be there, Inspector."

"Thank you, sir. I'm sure we'd all like to get this matter cleared up as soon as possible."

"Of course," Welles said.

Emerson nodded, and left.

Welles allowed a respectable amount of time to go by and then he called out, "George!"

Belson came running in.

"Yes, sir?"

"Get me Healy—now!"

When Leonard Roberts walked into the room, Karen Akers stood up quickly, rubbing her hands together nervously.

"Did you get it?"

The look on Roberts's face answered that question.

"No."

"What happened?"

"Never mind."

"What happened, Leonard?" she said, her tone demanding.

"I said never mind—"

"As you've told me so many times, I'm in this as deeply as you are," Karen argued. "I'd like to know what happened?"

He studied her for a few moments, then said, "All right. He wasn't there, and I had to kill the woman."

"You killed her?"

"She saw me, Karen, and she knew why I was there."

"But did you have to kill her?"

"Yes," Roberts said. "If I hadn't, she would have talked."

"To the police?"

"Or to Pike."

"The man who killed Bob Cole."

Roberts nodded and said, "That's right."

Karen had a sneaky suspicion that Pike hadn't killed Cole at all, but she didn't have the nerve to brave Roberts about it.

She wondered how long it was going to take him to decide to kill her? Maybe she was the one who should be talking to the police.

Or to this Jack Pike.

"What are we going to do now?" she asked.

"Now I go right to the source, and I cut out the middle man," Roberts said.

"Welles himself?" she asked.

"That's right."

"That's dangerous."

"No," Roberts said, pacing angrily, "you've got that wrong." He stopped, glared at her, and said, "I'm dangerous, and everyone is going to find that out—especially Mr. Richard Welles."

PART SEVEN

SHOWDOWN

CHAPTER TWENTY-TWO

Within the hour Healy was in Richard Welles's office. It was easy, because they both wanted to see each other.

"What the hell happened?" Welles snapped. "Pike is supposed to be dead, and instead he's finding Lila's body at my house."

"Lila's dead?"

"You didn't know?"

"There are a lot of things I didn't know," Healy said. "I think they know about me."

"Is that a fact?"

"I'm gonna need some money, Mr. Welles," Healy said. "I can't let them arrest me."

"If you bolt and run, they will arrest you," Welles said. "If they haven't done it by now, they must not have enough evidence."

"We can't be sure—"

"There's one way we can be sure, Healy."

"How is that?"

"Kill Pike."

"But Key and Wayne—"

"You're going to have to do it yourself," Welles said.

"Me? I can't—"

"You have to, Healy, or both of our careers—and our lives—will be over."

Healy felt sick to his stomach.

"It's up to you, Healy," Welles said. "It's all in your hands."

Healy fought to keep from throwing up and said, "I'll take care of it, Mr. Welles."

"You'd better."

Healy left, and Welles stood up. He knew he was going to have to go down to the undertaker's to identify Lila's body. He also knew that Pike was the only one to have seen him and Lila together in his house.

Healy had better be up to the job.

Pike, feeling that he'd given Emerson ample time to question Welles, left his hotel and headed back to the Welles house.

He hoped that what he found this time would be nothing like what he'd found the last time.

Leonard Roberts was worried about Karen Akers. Karen's expertise was working on rich men, bilking them out of some of their money. Murder was way beyond her capabilities, and she was starting to show signs of strain—like Cole.

Still, she was a beautiful woman, possibly the most beautiful Roberts had ever come across. It would be a shame to kill her, unless he absolutely had to.

Suddenly, unbidden, with the thought of killing her came a huge, pulsing erection. It was the same kind of erection he'd gotten after killing Jennifer Welles, while looking down at her naked body. Jennifer Welles had been a beautiful woman, and he realized for the first time how similar she and Karen were.

198

"What are you thinking about?" Karen asked.

Roberts suddenly felt embarrassed, as if she had caught him with his hands on his own penis.

"Nothing," he said, "just my next move."

"Which is?"

He looked at his watch and said, "I'm going to his house."

"Mr. Welles's?"

"Yes, Mr. Welles's," he said, testily, "who the hell else's house would I be going to?"

"What if he's not there?"

"He'll be there," Roberts said. "There's been just enough time for the police to question him. Pike is going to want to go back to the house to have a look."

"Why?" she asked, puzzled. "The police will have moved the body by now?"

Roberts laughed and said, "Morbid curiosity. He won't be able to resist going back to take a look."

"I don't know about this," Karen said.

"Nervous?" he asked.

She was nervous about admitting she was nervous. "It's just all this sitting around."

"Well then, don't sit around," Roberts said.

"What am I supposed to do?"

"Get dressed, girl," Roberts said. "You're coming with me."

"What?"

"You heard me," Roberts said, "get dressed."

His tone made it clear that it was not an invitation.

When Welles stepped inside his house he stopped just inside the door. He knew he'd been a fool to allow Lila to come to the house, but he'd missed her. With Jennifer dead and out of the way, he'd wanted to be with Lila as much as he could. He felt he was going to have to get his fill of her before he got into the governor's house, because once he was governor he was going to have to let her go.

He knew he should have felt some sense of loss. After all, he'd lost two women in one week, both of whom he'd been in love with at one time or another, both of whom he'd made love to at one time or another.

As good as both women were in bed, though, they paled next to his real lover—politics.

He moved away from the front door and climbed the stairs to the second floor. He didn't know why, but he had to see where Lila was killed. There was something . . . hypnotic about it, about her being killed in the same room where they had made love so many times.

He stopped in the upper hall for a moment, then took a deep breath, walked down the hall to the bedroom and stepped inside.

He started when he saw the man there, and almost cried out.

"I'm sorry," Jack Pike said, "I didn't mean to scare you."

"What the hell are you doing here?" Welles demanded. His vehemence betrayed just how frightened he had truly been by Pike's presence.

"I thought it was time we talked," Pike said. "I mean, really talked, without the lies."

"I never lied to you."

"You told me Lila was your sister."

"Lila told you she was my sister," Welles said. "I never said any such thing."

"You had your wife killed, didn't you, Welles?" Pike asked, deciding to be as direct as he could be. "You had my friend framed."

"This is ridiculous—"

"You had Lieutenant Healy hire two men to kill me," Pike went on. "You had a harmless little man named

200

Stilwell killed—"

"Stilwell?" Welles said, looking genuinely puzzled. "I don't know what you're—"

Pike was simply putting the blame for everything on Welles, to see how he'd react. It was probable that Welles was only responsible for some of it, but Pike just kept on going.

"You probably even had Lila killed—if that was her real name."

"It was," Welles said, "and this is all preposterous, Pike."

"She wasn't your sister."

"Of course she wasn't my sister," Welles said.

"She was your woman?"

"My mistress," Welles said.

"You had a beautiful wife," Pike said, "why would you need another—"

"Are you married, Pike?"

"No."

"Have you ever been?"

"No."

Wearily, Welles said, "Then you can't possibly understand what drives a man to take a mistress, no matter how beautiful his wife may be."

"I suppose not," Pike said, "but I can understand that more than I could understand a man having his wife killed."

"That's your surmise," Welles said. Pike didn't know what "surmise" meant, but he could guess.

"I can understand a man killing his wife," Pike said, "that I can understand, but paying someone to kill her? That I could never understand."

Welles stared at Pike for a few long moments, and Pike wondered if the man was going to confess.

When he spoke, however, it was not a confession.

"Get up," Welles said.

"What?"

"Get off the bed!"

Pike frowned, and stood up.

"Look, Welles—"

Richard Welles walked across the room and sat down on the bed, near one of the bed tables.

"Welles, the police know—"

"The police know nothing," Welles said, "just as you know nothing."

"You and I are the suspects in two murders, Welles," Pike said, "Steve Stilwell and Lila."

"Stilwell!" Welles said. "Inspector Emerson mentioned that name. I don't know anyone named Stilwell."

Pike studied Welles and was inclined to believe the man on this point. He did, however, still feel that Welles was responsible for the death of his wife, and the attempt on him.

"Tell me something, Welles."

"What?"

"What is it I know that would make you want to have me killed?"

Welles looked up at Pike from the bed.

"It's just the two of us here," Pike said. "I'd like to know."

Pike waited while Richard Welles made up his mind.

"If I wanted you killed," Welles finally said, "and I say 'if,' it would probably be because you were a threat to my career."

"How could I threaten your career?" Pike asked. "I came down from the mountains to talk to some men about furs."

"Furs," Welles said, shaking his head and laughing. "You came to St. Louis to talk about furs, and somehow your life became entangled with mine."

202

"Well," Pike said, "I'd like to untangle it. Tell me how?"

"It's too late," Welles said. He opened a drawer in the bed table before Pike could react and took out a small pistol. "It's much too late for that."

"Wait a minute—" Pike said.

"Take the pistol from your belt and toss it on the bed," Welles said.

"Welles—"

"Do it slowly."

Pike took hold of the pistol lightly, with two fingers, removed it and tossed it onto the bed. Welles left it there and ignored it.

"You're the only one," Welles said, "who can keep your friend from being convicted of murdering my wife."

"McConnell?"

"Those idiots," Welles said, impatiently. "They chose him because he looked like he was alone, only he wasn't. He had come here with you, and you wouldn't sit still while he was arrested for murder."

"He's my friend," Pike said.

"I understand that," Welles said, "believe me, I do. I understand about friendship. Those idiots I hired, they don't. They have no concept of what friendship is."

Pike's heart was racing, but he didn't know if it was because Welles was finally confessing, or because he was moments away from being killed.

Leonard Roberts and Karen Akers approached Welles's house.

"I don't like this," Karen said.

"I wanted you to come."

"Why?"

"Because," he said, "there was an alternative I didn't want to consider."

Karen shivered, because she thought she knew what that alternative was.

They approached the front door.

"How are we going to get in?" Karen asked.

"The way most people get into a house," Roberts said. "We'll knock."

Roberts did so, knocking loudly.

Upstairs, both Pike and Welles heard the knock.

"Now what do we do?" Pike asked.

"Shut up," Welles said.

"You think they'll go away?"

"I'm warning you—"

"Maybe it's the police."

That seemed to strike home. Welles licked his lips and his eyes darted from side to side. The knocking came again, and prompted him into action.

"All right," Welles said, "let's go downstairs."

"What are we gonna tell them, Richard?"

"Just move."

"Maybe it's just an assistant with some papers for you to sign," Pike said as they went down the hall.

"Shut up," Welles said, "or by God I'll kill you right here."

There was just enough tension in Welles's voice to convince Pike that he was on the edge of doing just that.

"Something's wrong," Roberts said, looking around uncomfortably. He had observed the house and its surroundings before approaching it, and had seen nothing amiss.

"So he's not home," Karen said. "Why don't we just leave?"

"He's home," Roberts said, still looking around. "He's got to be."

"Then what's wrong?"

"I don't know," Roberts said, "I don't know . . . yet." He turned to her and said abruptly, "Stay here."

"Where are you going?"

"Just stay here," he hissed.

"What if the door opens?"

He was moving away already, and he turned and said to her, "Be charming. You know how to do that."

CHAPTER TWENTY-THREE

Pike led the way to the front door. Welles was so close behind him that from time to time he felt the barrel of the gun poke him in the back. Still, Welles was wound up so tight Pike wasn't prepared to test him.

"Open it," Welles said.

"The knocking has stopped."

"Open it!"

Pike shrugged and opened the door. The woman on the doorstep had been looking behind her. When the door opened she gasped and turned around, momentarily stunning both men with her beauty.

"Well, hello," Pike said.

Her smile was tentative, forced as she said, "Uh, hello."

Before Pike could speak again Welles said, "Come inside."

"What?" she said.

Welles pointed the gun at her and said, "Come inside!"

"Better do as he says," Pike said. "He's very nervous right now."

She swallowed, nodded and entered.

"Close the door, Pike!" Welles said.

Pike closed the door.

"All right, let's go inside." To the woman he said, "You lead the way."

Karen Akers walked ahead of the two men, followed closely by Pike.

When they reached the living room Welles said, "All right, sit down."

The girl turned, looked at the gun and sat down. Pike wanted to remain standing. There wasn't much he could do from a seated position.

"Look, Welles, this is silly," Pike said. "The police know about you, they know about Healy, they know everything."

"Shut up!" Welles said. He turned to the woman and said, "Who are you?"

"M-my name is Karen."

"Karen what?"

"A-Akers."

"What are you doing here?"

No answer.

"Come on, what are you doing here?"

"Must you point that gun at me?" she asked. "It makes me nervous."

"Come on, Welles," Pike said, "we don't want to make the girl nervous, do we?"

"I'm sorry," Welles said, "but this man broke into my house. For all I know, you're working with him."

"I'm not," she said, "really."

"Who are you with?" Pike asked. Before she could answer, though, it came to him suddenly. "You're her."

"What?" she said.

"Who?"

"You're the girl who enticed my friend—Skins McConnell—out of the tavern."

"I don't know—" she started, but the look on her face said that she had been caught.

207

"What are you talking about?" Welles asked.

"This is the girl the real killers used to set up my friend."

Welles looked at Karen.

"Is that true?"

She didn't answer.

"Is it?" he demanded. "Look, Roberts works for me. Do you work with him? With Leonard Roberts."

Pike seized the name and memorized it.

The girl, growing panicky, began to look around as if she was looking for someone.

"He's here, isn't he?" Pike asked. "That's who you came with."

Now Welles was looking around.

"Why would he come here?"

"Have you paid him yet?" Pike asked.

The look on Welles's face answered that.

"You haven't."

"I haven't had a chance."

"So he came here earlier, looking to get paid, and found Lila. Was she in on it?" Pike asked. "Did she know you were having your wife killed?"

Welles opened his mouth, but nothing came out the first time.

"Yes," he said, having better success the second time, "she did."

"Something went wrong, and your Leonard Roberts killed her," Pike said. He looked at the girl and said, "He killed her, didn't he?"

"Y-yes," she said. "I didn't know—"

"And he killed Jennifer Welles?"

She lowered her head and said, "Yes."

"And you helped him set up my friend?"

"Yes."

"What are you gonna do now, Welles?" Pike asked. "Kill us both?"

Welles was sweating, moving the gun from one to the other and finally settling on Pike.

"And what about Roberts?" Pike asked. "He's here, somewhere. Outside the house, inside the house, here somewhere."

Welles looked around wildly.

"Roberts!" he shouted. "Roberts? Are you here? I've got your money. I'll pay you now!"

"Maybe he's too angry to be satisfied with getting paid," Pike said.

"No," Karen said, "he only wants the money."

"Roberts?" Welles shouted. "I'll pay you more than we agreed. Where the hell are you?"

"Here," a voice said, and a white-haired man holding a pistol stepped from the kitchen.

"Roberts," Welles said, and for that split second his attention was directed totally toward the hired killer.

Pike moved. He sprang from his seat, pushing Welles toward the kitchen. Roberts fired. Pike heard the shot, but didn't feel any pain so he kept on going. He headed for the stairs and ran up to the second floor. His gun was on the bed in Welles's bedroom, and his only chance of survival was to reach it.

When he reached the bedroom and grabbed the gun he realized that the weapon was not his full salvation, at all. There were two people—three, if he counted the woman—downstairs who had reasons to want him dead. Although carrying the pistol while he was in St. Louis, he was not carrying his powder horn or anything else he needed to reload.

He had one shot, and the knife that Welles had not realized he had.

Rather than try to get back downstairs, his best course of action was to escape. Welles had confessed to him, and he had both the killer's name, and the woman involved. He had enough to clear McConnell, and maybe even get himself clear of any charges.

That is, if he could get out of the house alive.

Pike decided not to run. It went against his nature. Besides, no one had chased him up the steps, and it was pretty quiet downstairs.

He moved out into the hall, his gun in his right hand. He left his knife sheathed for now. He inched his way down the hall, keeping his back against the wall, moving toward the head of the stairs.

When he reached the top of the stairs he paused and listened. There were no sounds from the floor below. He stepped down to the next step, and then listened. He moved down a few more and did the same. Finally, he was three quarters of the way down and could see the living room.

There was a man lying on the floor.

Still cautious, he came down the stairs the rest of the way and moved toward the body. Before crouching over it he looked toward the front foyer, and the kitchen. Finally convinced, leaned over the body and turned it over. It was Richard Welles, and he was dead. He'd been shot through the chest, probably with a ball that was meant for Pike.

After killing Welles, it looked like Leonard Roberts had left the house, taking Karen Akers with him.

Pike stared down at Welles and wondered how he was going to explain this to Inspector Emerson.

Pike left the house cautiously, just in case Roberts was waiting for him outside. When it became obvious that he was not, he went directly to the police station to talk to Emerson.

* * *

"Richard Welles, this time?" Emerson said. "You've gone too far, this time, Pike."

"I didn't kill him!"

"Who did?"

"A man named Leonard Roberts. He's the one Welles hired to kill his wife."

"Why?"

"I'm not sure. It might have been because Lila was his mistress, it might have been because she would have embarrassed him as a governor's wife. We didn't have a chance to get that straight. Welles pulled a gun on me, and then the woman arrived—"

"What woman?"

"Karen Akers," Pike said. "She's the one who lured McConnell into all this. After that Roberts stepped out from the kitchen, and then I ran for it."

"How did Welles get shot?"

"That may have been partially my fault," Pike said. "I pushed him toward Roberts just as Roberts fired at me."

"And he hit Welles instead."

"That's right."

Emerson sat back in his chair.

"Do you believe me?"

"Fortunately for you," Emerson said, "I recognize Roberts's name. Also, knowing that he's involved means that the man you found dead in the doorway was his partner, Robert Cole. Chances are Roberts killed him."

"What about Stilwell?"

"Stilwell must have been Mrs. Welles's most recent lover," Emerson said. "Roberts probably got to him— maybe using this Karen Akers—and used him to lure Jennifer Welles to that hotel."

"Then they went out to find a patsy, and Skins fell

into it."

"Right."

"Can you let him go now?"

"Not just like that," Emerson said. "Give all this information to his lawyer, he'll know what to do with it."

"Am I clear?"

"Cord Wayne is talking," Emerson said. "He's named Healy as the man who hired him and Key to kill you."

"How can you prove Healy was working for Welles?" Pike asked.

"We can't," Emerson said, "but once we get Healy, he'll give us Welles, especially since he's already dead."

"Can you catch Roberts?" Pike asked.

"Well, he'll want to get out of town. We'll try and cover every way he could leave. Your description is certainly good enough."

"And the woman?"

"My guess is he'll kill her," Emerson said. "He'll be able to move faster without her, and he won't want to leave her behind."

"What about Healy? Are you going to arrest him, now?"

"We'll bring him in and question him," Emerson said. "If he's smart, he'll confess."

"And if he doesn't?"

"We'll confront him with Wayne."

"So it's all wrapped up?"

"It is if everything happened the way you say it did," Emerson said. "This doesn't mean that you're free to leave town."

"I can't leave until I get this fur thing settled, anyway."

"Good, then I'll know where to find you."

"Okay."

Pike stood up and started for the door.

"Pike."

"Yeah?"

"The same men that might stop Roberts from leaving town could do the same to you."

"Don't worry," Pike said, "I'm not leaving."

Emerson smiled and said, "Glad to hear it."

CHAPTER TWENTY-FOUR

The next day Andy Dundee managed to get Skins McConnell released. Pike was waiting outside when Skins and Dundee came out.

"Jesus," McConnell said, "fresh air."

"As fresh as it can be away from the mountains," Pike said.

The two friends regarded each other for a moment, and then embraced warmly.

"Thanks," McConnell said. "I heard you almost got yourself a cell next to me trying to get me out."

"And he's not in the clear yet," Dundee said, "not until the police find the last three people in this puzzle—Healy, Leonard Roberts and Karen Akers."

"Karen," McConnell said, "that the gal who got me into this, isn't it?"

"It is," Pike said. "She was working with the two men who were the real killers."

"Two men?"

"Come on," Pike said. "We'll go to the hotel so you can clean up."

"After that I want a drink, a meal, and a woman."

"After that I'll buy you the drink and the meal and fill you in," Pike said. "The rest is up to you—just remember that a strange woman got you into this mess."

"I can't very well swear off women totally because of that, can I?" McConnell asked.

"No," Pike said, laughing, "I guess not."

Leonard Roberts thought about Karen Akers. It had really bothered him to have to kill a woman so beautiful, but he just couldn't take her along with him, she would have slowed him down—and he couldn't very well leave her behind. Once the decision had been made, however, killing her had been fairly easy. He had done it immediately after sex, squeezing her neck until she stopped wriggling.

Now Roberts was sitting in Jack Pike's room, waiting for the man to return. He meant to give Pike the same kind of surprise Pike must have given Richard Welles. Pike was the last order of business. Because Pike had been at Welles's house when Roberts arrived, Roberts had accidentally shot Welles. That done, he had never been paid for killing Jennifer Welles.

He was about to take his money's worth out of Jack Pike's hide.

Inspector Earl Emerson looked down at the body of Karen Akers. She was naked, but he was looking at her swollen tongue, which was sticking out of her mouth. The man had strangled her to death.

Undoubtedly, that man was Leonard Roberts. He knew Roberts's reputation as a reliable killer for hire, but the man seemed to have gone mad. He had done the same thing to Karen Akers that he had done to Jennifer Welles, and in between he'd killed his partner and his employer.

215

No one was ever going to hire Leonard Roberts again.

In a perverse way, Emerson figured Roberts might just blame Jack Pike for that.

"Come on," he told two of his men, "we're going to the Carlyle Hotel."

When Pike, McConnell and Dundee entered the lobby of the Carlyle Dundee said, "You two go up to your room. I'll wait in the bar. Since this case is over, I believe Pitch is behind the bar again."

"We'll join you in a little while," Pike said.

"Andy," McConnell called.

"Yeah?"

"Don't disappear, we've got some celebrating to do."

"I'll be there waiting, even though I didn't get to show off in court."

McConnell slapped him on the back and followed Pike up the stairs to the second floor while Dundee went into the bar.

Pike and McConnell were talking as they approached their room, alerting Roberts to the fact that they were coming. He sat in a straightbacked chair by the window, his pistol in his hand.

He heard the key scrape in the lock and then Pike entered the room, followed by McConnell.

"Good," Leonard Roberts said, "you're both here."

Pike stopped short as he saw Roberts, seated and pointing a gun at them.

"What the—" McConnell said. "What a welcome. Who is this guy, Pike?"

"This is the man who killed Jennifer Welles, Skins," Pike said. "Meet Leonard Roberts."

"You're the one who tried to frame me?"

216

"It was a good frame, too," Roberts said. "It would have worked, if it wasn't for your friend, here."

"I've already thanked him," McConnell said, taking a step toward Roberts. "Now I have to thank you."

Roberts raised the pistol and said, "Another move and I'll kill you."

"You do that," McConnell said, "and Pike will kill you."

Roberts frowned.

"And if you kill me," Pike said, "McConnell will kill you."

Roberts was still frowning. Actually, he'd only expected Pike, and that was why he had one pistol instead of two.

They had good points, he thought, and wondered which one he should shoot, and which he should kill with his bare hands.

Still watching Roberts, Pike began to move sideways, putting more room between himself and McConnell. There was no way Roberts could cover them both with one pistol. Pike's own pistol was on his belt. It was for that reason that he was sure Roberts would fire at him and not at Skins McConnell.

"Come on, Roberts," Pike said, "let's make a move here. We have some celebrating to do."

"Make up your mind, Roberts," McConnell said. "Do me a personal favor. Shoot Pike. I want to get my hands on you."

Inspector Earl Emerson and two of his men entered the lobby of the Carlyle Hotel and went directly to the front desk.

"Yes?" the clerk asked. "Can I help you?"

"Jack Pike's room," Emerson said.

"Oh, him?"

217

"Never mind the bull, sonny," Emerson said, "just give me the damned room number."

The clerk opened his mouth to reply, but they all heard a shot at that point.

"I'll bet that's it," the clerk said.

"What floor?" Emerson demanded.

"Second," the clerk called after the policeman, who was already leading his men up the steps.

The ball from Roberts's pistol struck Pike in the belly, and he fell to the floor.

McConnell moved as soon as Roberts fired, and was on the man incredibly fast. Roberts had no time to set himself. He tried to swing at McConnell with the empty gun, but the mountain man fended the blow off with an elbow and closed his hands on the man's neck, lifting him from the chair.

Leonard Roberts considered himself a fine fighter, and felt he could hold his own with anyone, and beat most. He'd fired at Pike not because the man was armed, but because he was the bigger of the two. He'd felt sure he could defeat McConnell hand to hand. He had not counted on the man's anger exploding, doubling his strength.

He felt himself lifted from the chair by the throat. He finally got the pistol free from between their bodies and clubbed McConnell with it, but the mountain man didn't seem to feel the blows.

Spots began to form before Roberts's eyes and he felt his body begin to be deprived of air.

He knew he was a dead man.

As Emerson exploded into the room, pistol in hand, he saw Pike on the floor. In front of the window he saw

Skins McConnell holding Leonard Roberts by the throat, and Roberts's feet were not touching the ground.

"McConnell!" he shouted. "Let him go!"

Skins McConnell did not hear him.

"McConnell, damn it, I want him alive!"

There was still no indication from McConnell that he heard anything as he continued to squeeze the life out of the man who had almost successfully framed him for murder.

"McConnell," Emerson shouted, "don't make me shoot."

McConnell also thought that Pike was belly shot, and that was even more reason for him to kill the man whose neck he was crushing.

"Skins!" Pike shouted. "I'm all right! Let him go, we need him alive."

McConnell heard Pike's voice and paused. He didn't release the pressure on Roberts's neck, but he was no longer squeezing quite as hard.

"Skins, let . . . him . . . go!" Pike shouted.

"I'll have to club him," Emerson said, "or shoot him."

McConnell heard that. Abruptly, he opened his hands and Roberts fell to the floor, gasping for air, holding his damaged throat.

McConnell turned to Pike, who had staggered to his feet, still holding his belly. There was some blood, but not as much as one would have expected from a belly shot.

"What the hell—" McConnell said. "I thought you were gutshot."

"So did I," Pike said. He removed his hands from his belly and they both saw the shattered and splintered wood of his damaged Kentucky pistol. The splatters of blood came from wooden splinters that had entered the flesh of Pike's belly.

"Damned thing saved my life," Pike said. He pulled the remainder of the gun from his belt and dropped it to the floor.

McConnell looked around the room to where Emerson and his two policemen were assisting Leonard Roberts to his feet.

"Ah, to hell with freshening up," he said. "Let's go get that drink and celebrate."

Pike, picking splinters from his belly, said, "I'm for that."

EPILOGUE

There was quite an entourage to accompany Pike and McConnell to the train station the following week.

Inspector Earl Emerson was there. Pike had caused so much trouble that he wanted to make sure the man got on the train;

Joe Pitch and Andy Dundee were there.

Charlie Sullivan was there. Danny wanted to be there, too, but he was not quite recovered sufficiently to leave the hospital.

Irma, the blond whore, was there. She had come to Pike's room a few days earlier, and when Pike told her he'd be leaving and when she said she'd come to see him off. True to her word, she did.

"I'll bet you'll be glad to get back to your mountains," Joe Pitch said to both of them.

"You can still come along, Joe," Pike said.

"I'm tempted, but I think I'll stay in the city a little while longer."

"Hey," Dundee said, "what happened with those fur companies?"

Pike and McConnell exchanged glances. Pike had spoken to a new man at Hudson Bay, and had gone to the other two companies again, as well.

"They all said they'd consider my pleas," Pike said, "but that they could guarantee nothing."

"I guess we'll just have to go back and see what happens," McConnell said.

"Well, I wish you luck," Dundee said.

Pike and McConnell shook hands all the way around. Pike slipped some money into Charlie's hand during a handshake and said, "I guess you'll have to handle the money for a little while, Charlie."

"Thanks, Pike."

"And don't forget to go and see Dundee when Danny gets out of the hospital," Pike said. "He's got jobs for the both of you."

"Yes, sir."

Pike turned and caught Irma in midair, kissing her soundly.

"I won't forget you, Jack Pike."

Pike kissed her again and put her down.

As the train pulled out of the station Pike could see Irma standing close to Joe Pitch.

"She won't forget you, all right," Skins McConnell said, laughing. "Joe Pitch'll help her remember."

"I hope he enjoys her as much as I did," Pike said.

They sat back and prepared for their long journey.

"You know something?" McConnell said.

"What?"

"I don't mind this contraption so much now that I know it's taking me back to the mountains."

"There's good in all things, Skins," Pike said, "remember that."

"I'll remember."

After they had ridden a while McConnell said, "You know what I can't figure?"

"What's that?"

"What happened to that policeman, Healy."

"He must have used some of his contacts to get out of

222

the city," Pike said. "His career as a policeman, and his future as a politician, are both gone. I guess he'll just spend the rest of his life running and hiding."

"I guess," McConnell said. "Helluva way to live, though."

"There's worse ways," Pike said, looking at his friend. "You almost found that out yourself."

"Amen," Skins McConnell said, putting his head back and closing his eyes, "amen."

GREAT BOOKS

E-BOOKS

AUDIOBOOKS

& MORE

Visit us today

www.speakingvolumes.us